Mick Jamieson? 'A ra[...]
teacher. 'A boy like th[...]

But Penny, new to teaching, is undaunted and thinks that Mick is perfect for the part of the Artful Dodger in the school's production of the musical *Oliver* which she is helping to produce. What Penny doesn't know is that Mick's mum died three years ago, he hasn't got over it yet and his dad, a long-distance truck driver who is always away, doesn't seem to care.

Right up until the opening night, Mick is unsure that he will actually go through with it although he's learnt his lines and enjoyed the rehearsals.

Interwoven with Mick's story are the letters Penny writes to her friend about him. If Mick fails, she fails too . . .

Libby Gleeson movingly reveals the events of Mick's past that lead to a memorable crisis in the life of a young boy everybody thought was only a dodger.

Libby Gleeson was born in New South Wales, one of six children. After studying history at Sydney University, she spent five years in Italy and London. It was then that she started writing. On returning home she first taught in high school then in adult education. Now she is a full-time writer and lives with her husband and three daughters in Sydney. Her first novel for young readers, *Eleanor, Elizabeth* (also available in Puffin), was the winner of the Angus & Robertson Writers for the Young Fellowship and was Highly Commended in the 1985 Children's Book Council Awards. Her second novel, *I am Susannah*, was a 1988 Honour Book in the Children's Book Council Awards.

Also by Libby Gleeson

ELEANOR, ELIZABETH

Dodger

LIBBY GLEESON

PUFFIN BOOKS

This book was written with
the assistance of
the Literature Board of Australia

Lines from the musical *Oliver*
are quoted with kind permission
of Essex Music of Australia Pty Ltd
on behalf of
Lakeview Music Publishing Co Ltd, UK

PUFFIN BOOKS

Published by the Penguin Group
Penguin Books Ltd, 27 Wrights Lane, London W8 5TZ, England
Penguin Books USA Inc., 375 Hudson Street, New York, New York 10014, USA
Penguin Books Australia Ltd, Ringwood, Victoria, Australia
Penguin Books Canada Ltd, 10 Alcorn Avenue, Toronto, Ontario, Canada M4V 3B2
Penguin Books (NZ) Ltd, 182–190 Wairau Road, Auckland 10, New Zealand

Penguin Books Ltd, Registered Offices: Harmondsworth, Middlesex, England

First published by Turton & Chambers 1990
Published in Puffin Books 1992
1 3 5 7 9 10 8 6 4 2

Text copyright © Libby Gleeson, 1990
All rights reserved

The moral right of the author has been asserted

Printed in England by Clays Ltd, St Ives plc

For Euan

Cool dark place. Cement floor. Under the washtubs. Loud voices. A door slams. Cars start up. The boy presses his face down hard against his knees. They're all gone now. He looks up slowly. Mrs Jackson from across the road bends down and peers in at him. Come on, love, she says. Come on out of there. It won't solve nothing, you know, hiding away like this. He doesn't answer. You come out and have a bite to eat. They'll be hours. You'll be starving hungry by the time your dad gets back. Still he doesn't answer. He looks at her calmly. She frowns for a moment. Come on out now. She almost kneels on the laundry floor. She holds her arms out to him as if he were a baby. Come and have a good cry.

He presses his back against the cold, hard cement and closes his eyes.

It is dark. The man lifts the boy down from the truck. He stumbles when his feet hit the ground. Come on, love. It's Nanna here. You haven't forgotten me, have you? What a big boy you are now, you're nearly past my shoulder and you've come all the way to see me. Come in where it's warm. I bet you're tired. That was such a long drive. She puts her arm across his shoulders. He is too tired to shrug it off as she pushes him to the warm light of the kitchen. He tries to stay awake. The gas fire glows in the corner of the lounge room. He sits on the sofa and leans towards the voices in the hallway . . .

I had to bring him down to you, Mum. I didn't know what else to do . . . he won't cry. He says nothing. I think he understands that she's not coming back. I can't work it out. I don't know what he understands.

He slips sideways onto the soft cushion. He feels in his pocket for his watch. His fingers close tightly over it. Fractured dreams of soap smells, voices, a cool dark place, cement floor.

BOY

School tomorrow. Two more years. Eight terms. How many weeks is that? Can't be bothered working it out. Too many anyway. Hope we get some decent new teachers. Hope Masterman's been given the boot. Bet he hasn't. Tom reckons he's wagging first day. Going up to Liverpool to play the machines. Says his mum don't care. Nan does though. Same story every morning . . . got your lunch . . . got your homework . . . go and do your hair . . . tuck your shirt in. When Dad comes back, he won't make me.

TEACHER

School tomorrow. Hope the kids are nice . . . and the staff. Wish someone else from our year had been appointed with me. Hope it doesn't take too long to find a place to live. Might be someone good to share with. Hope the boss is OK. Hope they don't dump all the rotten classes on the new teachers. Be awful if I just get to yell at kids all day. I won't, won't, won't end up like that. How on earth am I going to remember everything?

One

The boy lies in the dirt under the oleander and
watches the road. He smells the truck and hears the
gears grind through the changes at the bottom of the
hill. Come on. Like Dad says. Just a bit more effort.
He stretches forward. He can almost see it. A Mack.
Not Dad's. Different sound completely. Silver
letters scrawled across the front grille. Two huge red
containers on the tray. It gathers speed, pulls out
around and above a tiny white Datsun. The boy
pushes himself up onto his knees. The truck and car
run parallel. The truck's horn blares. The car slows
and pulls further to the left. Its front wheel spins on
gravel. Tiny stones fly up and into the grass. The
boy grips the fence. Come on. The car and truck are
level. Then the truck pulls further forward. The
second container passes the car. Come on. Grey
smoke pours from the stack. Nearly there. The boy is
on his toes. He lets go of the fence, clenches both
fists. His broken nails tear his palms. Come on.
Come on. The truck cuts in front and hits the top of
the hill. He leaps in the air, waving one fist above
him, and falls back, rolling in the grass as the bell
rings.

Mick pushed the door open with his toe and stepped
inside.

My Personal History.

A new teacher was at the board, underlining the heading.

Mick slid his bag across the back of the desks till it collided with Tom's foot and then he moved towards his seat, elbows and hips knocking into chairs.

'Watch it, Jamieson.'

'Watch it yourself.'

As Mick pulled out the chair next to Tom's, the teacher slowly put the cap back onto the pen and stepped forward. Mick frowned and bent down to pick up his bag.

'Michael Jamieson, I presume?' She raised one eyebrow.

'Mick, miss. Everyone calls me Mick.' He grinned and looked at Tom and Danny, who turned to the board.

'Well, Mick, I'd like you to come out here. I want to speak to you.' She sat back on the desk and waited.

Mick paused for a moment. He kept grinning at Tom and Danny, Alex and the others around the back table. A few glanced up from their writing. He scraped his chair back slowly as far as the wall, and stood up.

The teacher didn't say anything. She watched as he walked between the desks.

'Think ya cool,' whispered Trent Taylor.

The teacher tapped the board. 'Get on with your work.' She moved to talk to Mick so that her back was to the class and they couldn't hear her words. He put his hands in his pockets and looked at the floor.

'Some teachers,' she said slowly, folding her arms, 'might ask you why you are late. But I'm not going to do that.'

Mick looked up. The sun was coming through the window behind her. It meant he couldn't see her face properly. It made him squint and look away.

'Are you wearing a watch?' She tapped the face of hers with her fingernail.

'Yeah, miss. Never take it off.' He held his arm out and pointed to the black leather band.

'Well, use it.'

Mick shifted his weight from one leg to the other.

'It's the first time we've met and I don't intend to rant and rave. Just don't let it happen again.'

'No, miss.' Mick turned to go.

'And another thing.' She waited till he faced her again. 'If it does happen, you don't just walk in and go straight to your desk. It's disruptive to everyone. They're trying to work. You should apologize to the whole class.'

Mick shrugged and looked around the room. Tom was leaning back on his chair, tapping the edge of the desk with his pen. Trisha and Alex were talking quietly, not looking to the front. Debbie was examining the ends of the long plait that hung over her shoulder while, next to her, Anya cleaned her fingernails with a silver nail file. Cheryl and Tammy were writing and Chris just stared out the window. Mick looked at the teacher.

'Aw, miss. They don't care.'

'What did she say?' said Tom.

'Nothing.' Mick opened his bag. Two cheese and tomato sandwiches wrapped in brown paper and a Biro. 'Give us a bit of paper, Tom.' He looked at the board.

My Personal History.

'What's she on about?' He leant across and looked at Tom's folder where he had written the heading and underneath it:

Date of birth – February 14th. 1977.

'What are we s'pose to do?' Mick looked at the board again and then back at Tom. 'And what's *Penny* written up there for?'

'That's her. Her name.'

'Are we s'pose to call her that?'

Tom nodded and kept writing.

'Crawler.'

Under the major heading on the board was a list of words.

Birth?
School?
Family?
Important Events?
?? ????

The teacher, Penny, had moved to the window. She bent over the desk where Sharon and Carla sat, and talked to them in a low voice. Mick could see, through the window behind her, a blur of black tee shirts. Kids running the torture track – three wide circuits while Masterman bellowed. Then beyond them the reserve, the long spread of bushes and the freeway. That truck wasn't Dad's. He's out there though. Tape music blares. Rows of lights gleam on wet tar.

He jumped. She was squatting beside him. He looked straight at the bouncy orange curls and the chipped front tooth. She tapped the desk top with an orange fingernail.

'What you're doing,' she said, 'is making notes on your personal history. Before we start lessons for the year, I want you to think about what history means to you.'

Mick looked at the blank sheet of paper.

'It's nothing to me, miss.'

'Just start with who you are and where you come from. Where you were born. When. Your life to date. Whatever important things have happened to you.'

'Nothing important ever happens here. Not to us.' He dug Tom in the ribs. 'Eh, Tom? Except when a truck goes over at the bottom bend and dumps its load and you can get all the stuff you can carry away for free.'

She looked like she was going to say something but didn't. She stood up and clapped her hands. 'Just a couple more minutes and then it'll be time to talk about it.'

*

'I was born at Liverpool Hospital in nineteen seventy-seven. Mum was born in Australia but Dad and all my grandparents were born in Greece.' Chris looked up from his paper. 'You guys know all this stuff.' He shrugged his shoulders and continued. 'I've got two younger sisters, and the best thing that happened to me was when we all went back to Greece at the end of year six and we had a whole term off school. I met lots of relations and we travelled on a boat out to the island where one family of cousins lives. It was great and I'm going to go again when I leave school.'

'I was born in the country, in Wagga,' said Debbie Nichols. 'We left there when I was ten and came here. I've got one brother and we fight all the time. That's as much as I got.'

Penny was standing by the doorway listening to Trisha's group. She came over as Tom began.

'I was born in Sydney in nineteen seventy-seven. There's just me at home now because my big brother's gone to Wollongong to work. There's Mum and Dad too. The best thing was when we built our new house. I got to help Dad and all his mates do it. One of them's a brickie and I'm going to get an apprenticeship with him when I leave school in a couple of years.'

Penny nodded to Mick.

'I haven't got nothing,' he said.

'You don't need notes. You can tell us the same things as the others did. When were you born?'

'December. Nineteen seventy-seven.'

'Where?'

'Brisbane.'

'Don't you remember anything about being there?'

'No.' He shook his head.

Cold cement floor. The door bangs. Michael, Michael, where are you?

'And when did you come to Sydney to live?'

'Three years ago. When I was ten.'

'Well, you'd remember the move then. What was it like coming here to the big city? And your family. Mum? Dad? Did they move here for work? Or for family reasons?'

'Dunno. Mum's dead.'

'Oh, I'm sorry.'

Mick shrugged. 'That's all right. That's why we moved. Dad drives a truck. I live with Nan. He sort of still lives up there. He comes home sometimes. Sometimes I . . .'

She was smiling, raising her eyebrows. Waiting for him to go on.

'Nothing.'

'Can't you think of anything really special that has happened in your life?'

'No.'

'Come on.' She grinned and he noticed the chipped tooth again. She leant towards him. 'There must be something.'

'No, miss. Nothing.'

'Got any new teachers?' Nan pushed a plate of biscuits across the table.

'Couple.' Mick took a handful and swung his chair back so that it balanced on one leg.

'What are they like?'

'All right. History teacher's making us do all this stuff. You know. Where you come from.' He was chewing as he spoke and crumbs fell down the front of his shirt.

'You mean like if you've got convicts way back?' Nan looked up.

'No. Just us. Where we were born. Not real history. Not the olden days. Sort of like why we live here now. Stuff like that.'

'What did you tell her?'

'Nothing much. Not much to tell really.'

You'd remember the move then. And your family. Mum? Dad?

'D'you know when Dad's coming back through here?'

His grandmother shook her head. 'You asked me the other day. I told you then I didn't know. I never know.' She sipped her tea and didn't look up at him.

He went across to the window. The paint on the windowsill was cracked and he scratched it till a piece lifted. 'I'm going out for a while, OK?'

'Are you going over to that Tom's?'

'Dunno.'

'Haven't you got some homework to do?'

He was already at the door. 'They never give you anything on the first day.'

Mick went down the street past Petersens', Lees' and Calvaros's. Nick Calvaros was sitting on his

12

front fence. His bike lay across the driveway.

'Wanna go for a ride?' he said.

Mick shook his head and kept walking. He sometimes took his bike in the afternoon when he rode over past Tom's place or just around looking for something to do. But the paintwork was really rusty now and the front wheel was punctured. He hadn't fixed it at the weekend even though he had meant to.

He was heading for the new houses that sprawled along the freeway. Tom lived there, but when Mick got to the street you turn down to get to the Simmons' place, he kept walking. Past the primary school and the little shopping centre where he came to get the milk and the bread, past the video shop and the Baptist Church. He saw Mrs Calvaros on her way home from the bus stop. She crossed the street and waited for Trisha Allyson's mother, who was coming out of the butcher's. They looked at Mick and then looked away. He pushed his hands down into his pockets and started to jog.

The road forked and he crossed over and started uphill, up the slope that took him high over the freeway. His feet burned through his joggers. Eight lanes of traffic roared beneath him. Sydney to Melbourne. One hundred and twenty kilometres per hour. He breathed in the smell of diesel. At the top of the bridge he sat, feet dangling through the rails. On a clear day you could see the city, across twenty-five kilometres of suburbs. You could see planes circling over the airport, smoke pouring from the chimney stacks of the chemical plant along the river and, on the horizon, the jagged towers of the city proper. Today, the thick brown haze of summer heat and smog covered them all.

He looked down. He was right above the median strip. It was planted with small shrubs and they were bent and tossed about by the rushing of air after each car and truck. He watched a red spot in the distance. It grew larger and larger, a Porsche with the top down, probably 180 ks. It flashed beneath him. He saw the driver lift her hand to brush a hair away from her face. Her passenger had a map spread across his knees. Heading off? Canberra? Melbourne?

He's somewhere on the road. Sometimes he comes home to us. Remember the move. Remember . . .

Mick leant against the rails. Hot metal pressed against his cheeks and through his thin shirt. He stared at a blur until it turned into a BP tanker and three huge double tray semis. They passed beneath him. A horn blared. A long grey Commodore charged down the outside and cut sharply across in front of a yellow Renault.

'Stupid bastard.' Mick stood up and started to walk home.

Dear Fran:

Greetings from the outer western suburbs.
As you can see from the address, I'm in a
hotel for the moment but believe me, that's
only temporary. As soon as school settles
into some kind of a routine, I'll be out flat
hunting. There might even be someone on
the staff who I can share with.

Thanks for the card which was on my desk
when I started this morning. It was good to
know that someone was thinking of me! I
only wish I'd thought to send you one. I
couldn't believe how nervous I was. I
thought it would be just like doing a prac
but it wasn't. Somehow it all suddenly felt
so important and I was so responsible and I
had this overwhelming feeling that if I didn'
get it right first go then I never would.

That all sounds a bit heavy and of course
it wasn't really like that. Most of the
classes I got were fine. The best was
probably a year seven English. They were
all madly enthusiastic and of course they
didn't know I was new. Year eight history
kids, on the other hand, are a bit too cool
for that, and one in that group really got

to me. It's hard to say why. Cocky little kid, sauntered in late, headed for the back corner and he couldn't have cared less about my talking to him. At one stage it got a bit embarrassing. I was doing that preliminary exercise on personal history and I got them to talk about themselves and their stories. It turned out his mother is dead, his father is away in Brisbane and he lives down here with his grandmother. When I mentioned it in the staffroom at lunch-time, all the response I got was that loads of the kids come from more screwed up backgrounds than that.

Anyway, like I said, he got to me and I intend finding out more about him.

Enough of my day. Write and tell me all about yours. What classes did you score? Have you got anywhere to live? Is life on the coast as good as everyone makes out?

Right now I am missing you and the old house in Newtown so much. I might as well be on the moon - not hanging around in the fringe suburbs! Remember those nights we sat up till all hours, music playing, solving the problems of the world? It all seems so far away now.

Write soon. Love, Penny

Two

'What's this, Jamieson? No gear again today? Starting the year the same way we finished last year?' Mr Masterman strode around the change room and stopped in front of Mick. 'Come on. On your feet.'

'It's not my fault . . . ' Mick started.

'Don't give me that routine. I wasn't born yesterday. Out. Outside with the rest of them.' He banged on the door of the toilets. 'Out, you stragglers. Get moving!'

Mick followed the rest of the class onto the oval. The only one in jeans. He stood on the edge of the group – twenty boys all in shorts and joggers. Tom was in the middle pretending to have a punch-up with Danny Brett. They were both bigger than any of the others, and Danny reckoned he used his father's razor every weekend.

Mick's jeans felt hot and tight. There was sweat in the hair at the back of his neck and running down between his knees.

'OK. OK. Let's move it. What are we waiting for? Twice round and no slacking.' Masterman bounced up and down on the balls of his feet and the muscles on his thighs stood out. He wore short satin shorts, pulled tight. Mick knew that behind his fancy sunglasses, he was looking at him.

'I couldn't bring my shorts. Nan put them in the wash. I've only got one pair.'

'I haven't washed them yet,' Nan had said. 'Get them out and wear them one more time.' But he was late for the bus and forgot.

Mick looked straight at the mirrored glass hiding Masterman's eyes and saw his own face looking back. The glasses had red rims and the colour was repeated on the logo on the PE teacher's sleeveless tee shirt and the stripe down his right thigh. Must have cost a fortune.

'Is that the way to speak to a teacher?'

'No.'

'No, what?'

'No, sir.'

Mick folded his arms and looked down at the grass, burnt off by the sun. One of his shoelaces had broken in the rush this morning and was tied across only half its holes.

'And stand up straight when I'm talking to you. Shoulders back. Eyes to the front.'

Mick drew his breath in slowly, dropped his hands to his sides and waited. Chris Pappas was bent down, tying his shoelaces. He grinned at Mick behind Masterman's back. Then he set off with the stragglers. Tom and Danny were already more than halfway round. They liked PE. Were big enough to play in the forwards. Could keep up with anything that Masterman invented.

Mick turned back from them. Out of the corner of his eye he saw Penny walk around the side of the library building. She saw the boys running on the oval and she grinned as she leant back against the wall, in the shade, to watch.

Masterman walked behind Mick, poking him in the soft flesh of his back and shoulders. 'You're lucky, Jamieson. You're so lucky I could kill myself laughing.' He moved in front of him, folded his arms, unfolded them, put both hands on his hips and leant forward. 'Teachers like me aren't allowed to use the cane any more.' He was so close, Mick smelt a mixture of sweat and aftershave. 'I'd love to get my hands properly on a worm like you. Except you're hardly worth it. You've got an excuse for everything.' He straightened up and brushed his blond hair off his face. 'Don't you blame your old Nan for everything. It's your attitude, son. You don't care.'

Mick looked back towards the buildings. Penny wasn't grinning any more. She'd taken a few steps towards them and was staring at Masterman.

'You're cheeky. You don't pay any attention. You don't listen. You don't do as you are told.' His suntanned finger pressed hard against Mick's chest. 'You're a bloody nuisance and in a couple of years someone is going to be expected to employ you. So I've got that much time to smarten you up, make a decent citizen of you. Now get over there with the rest of them and run. Run, I said.'

He pushed Mick so hard that he stumbled against a pile of school bags and almost fell.

'Oh, sir.'

'One more whine out of you and it'll be three times round, then four, then five.' Masterman was screaming at him. 'I'll make you run all lesson.'

Mick started to jog. His jeans caught him, tight

and hot behind the knee. His hair fell into his eyes. He tossed his head to flick it back.

'Come on, Jamieson, lift those feet.' Masterman pounded alongside him, arms pumping. Mick gulped and tried to get into a stride. His chest hurt. Sweat poured down his face.

She wasn't standing by the building any longer. She was walking quickly across the playground to the administration block. Mick kept his eyes on the grass ahead. A green and brown blur. Masterman was ahead of him now, running strongly to where the others were bunched, almost back to the start.

In the middle of the oval, the girls were exercising – bending, stretching, touching their toes. Mick heard them calling to each other and laughing. Mrs Cooper was doing the movements with them. She was no taller than they were, and at times it was hard to see which was the teacher and which the students.

Mick was into a rhythm now but breathing heavily. Sweat ran down the side of his nose and into his open mouth. He tasted salt. Yuk. He closed his eyes for a moment.

From across the grass came Masterman's voice. 'I don't care how hot it is, I said twice round. Now move it.'

To Mick's right, beyond the shrubs and fences, was the road. The tops of the cars were just visible as he ran. A truck was coming up the hill. He listened, his head slightly to one side. A Mack? No. Mercedes? Dad? The thudding of his feet and his panting meant he couldn't quite hear. He wanted to stop, run from the oval, lean on the fence and watch as whatever it was came powering up the hill. He rounded the curve in the running track. He could hear the others behind him.

'Come on, you lot. You're all going to lap Jamieson.'

He felt the teacher drawing closer. Danny Brett came alongside first. Then Trev. Then Tom.

'Slacko, mate,' Tom said.

Words formed in Mick's brain but he couldn't say them. His chest hurt and he breathed in short sharp bursts. Sweat stung his eyes. They were coming up to the point where they had started. Masterman flashed past him, caught up with Tom's group and was chasing Danny and Trev. Racing flat out, pumping his arms, extending his stride. Mick puffed and slowed. They were all panting. They fell into a heap under the trees. Mick flopped, last, onto the spiky dry grass, cool in the shade.

'What do you think you're on about, Jamieson? The rest – take five. You, lad, have only been round once. Come on. On your feet. Again.'

At lunchtime, Mick walked behind Tom and Danny across the playground. Their bags dragged at their feet. They cut through a year seven handball game and waited for Trev as he came out of the canteen. He handed Tom a bottle of juice and a packet of chips.

'Juice's all they had left.'

Tom shrugged and led the way up behind the boys' toilets. They sprawled on the grass and Mick pulled out a paper bag of sandwiches. Cheese and tomato again.

Trev was talking to Tom. ' . . . and Masterman reckons we should both try out when the season starts. He reckons if we go for it we could make the zone team as well. You too Danny . . . He says . . . '

'Masterman's a bastard,' Mick said.

'What d'you expect if you didn't bring your stuff? You know what he's like.'

'He'd've found something else. He just likes picking on people.' Mick rolled away from them up on his elbows to finish his sandwich. 'Least he can't belt you any more.'

' . . . anyway. He reckons we should try out.' Trev stood up. 'He told me all about this girlfriend he's got . . . '

'He's just sucking up to you, Trev.' Mick looked away.

'You're just jealous because you don't get on with him.' Trev left to go to cricket practice.

Tom passed the last of his chips to Danny.

'Mum's gone up to Newcastle to my aunty's place. Dad and me are on our own this weekend. He reckons I can help him at work on Saturday, and on Sunday we might go out to the dam or down the coast to go fishing. Should be great. Want to come?'

'Yeah,' said Danny. 'Mum'll let me. Glad to get rid of me.' He blew into the chip bag and smashed it hard against the palm of his hand.

'My dad's coming home this weekend,' said Mick. 'Friday night. Probably go off again straightaway, but . . . '

'You always reckon he's coming,' said Tom. 'How come we never see him?'

Mick shrugged. 'He never stays in one place for long. Always working. Next holidays, he reckons he's going to take me back to Queensland.'

Dear Fran:

Good to get your letter last week and to
hear all your news. Being in such a small
school must be great. Sometimes I think I'll
never get to know everyone here. Good luck
with the house hunting. I've found something. I'm about to move into a house with
one of the music teachers - Bella Mitchell.
She's found a big old place a few blocks
away from the school and she needs someone else to join her. I think we'll get on
all right. There's a spare room so if you
get the urge to come for a weekend or a
bit of the holidays ...

Remember that kid I told you about, the
little bloke in year eight that really got to
me? Well I decided to follow him up and I
had a long talk to Gordon Richards about
him. Gordon's a senior English teacher and
co-ordinator of year eight and he seems
pretty good. Anyway, he started by telling
me not to worry and then when he saw I
wasn't going to be fobbed off, he pulled
out the record cards. They didn't say much.
The kid is bright but not achieving which
is what I had already worked out for
myself. There was a note about his family

circumstances, but just that, a note stating what they are.

Gordon reckons there are dozens of kids around with similar problems to Mick's and they are better off if they are left alone to grow up without us putting too many hassles in their way. Gordon's pretty laid back as you can tell. Part of me agrees with him. Another part of me says that that is a bit of a cop-out. There must be something we can do.

The one thing I do know for sure is that I don't agree with the philosophy of this other guy on the staff who teaches PE, called Masterman would you believe! When he's not head of the card playing set in the staffroom, he's putting into practice the belief that what the average weedy thirteen-year-old needs is a good run round the oval in the hot sun. The first time I saw him in action, I went charging up to the boss's office to complain. Neither she nor the Assistant Principal was in and, by the time I saw them, I'd calmed down and decided to hold my tongue. That kid, Mick, was one of the ones made to sweat.

To cap it all, I heard Masterman sounding off to a couple of the other new teachers about how the school lacked discipline and how all kids needed to be made to, quote,

`smarten up, toe the line and show respect'.
He ought to talk. What he means is `do as I
say and don't think for yourself'. How
depressing.

On that note, I'll get back to some marking,

Love,
Penny

P.S. Bella wants to do a school musical. She
says she'll be musical director and I can be
producer. The only time I've ever been on
stage was in a chorus when I was fourteen.
She says that's no excuse!

Three

'We have been talking,' said Penny, 'about ourselves and our personal histories.' She frowned at Mick, who was still reaching in his bag for his folder. 'Come on, Mick. I'm grateful that you're on time but I'd appreciate it if I had your complete attention.'

The last two words sounded like she had underlined them. He dropped his bag and kicked it under the desk.

'We're going to continue this week by looking at our local area.' She waved her hand towards her table, which was covered with books and folders. They rested in a large metal tray and spilled over onto the chair and the floor. Leaning against the wall were two shovels, a huge sheet of plastic and a couple of buckets.

'No history around here,' said Tom.

Penny raised her eyebrows. 'You'd be surprised. You might have noticed that I have all this . . . this stuff with me.'

'Going to do some digging, miss?'

'Could get some old bones?'

'Dead dogs, probably.'

'Not exactly. We're going to do some research into the local area and we're going to build a model of what it was like here about a hundred years ago. Now, how do you think we can go about doing this?

Who has any suggestions?'

'Look up some books.'

'Ask someone old.'

'Ask Mick's nan.'

'Look up old newspapers.'

Penny held up her hands. 'OK. OK. All of that. And some more. I'll write them on the board while you get into groups of about four or five people. Move quietly.'

'Now,' she said when she had finished. 'See if there's an activity that you would like to do. We're going to mix them around over the next few lessons so you won't get stuck forever on something you don't like.' She went across to the books and began sorting them into three separate piles.

Mick moved across the room to join Tom and Danny.

'I'm not reading books,' he said.'It's boring. And I'm not asking Nan. If you ask her a question about the old days, she says they were awful and she doesn't want to talk about them.'

'Would you boys like to go and get the dirt to make the ground?' called Penny.

'I want to look at those newspapers,' said Chris. 'It's too hot out there.'

'Come on,' said Tom. 'We could get out of class for half the lesson. We'd have to go right down the back behind the car park. Come on.' He stood up.

Chris stayed in his seat.

'Suit yourself,' said Tom.

Mick and Danny followed him out to the front.

'We'll get the dirt,' said Tom. 'We know a good place.'

'OK.' Penny nodded. 'Don't take all day, will you?'

'No, miss,' said Mick.

They crossed the playground and came up to the boys' toilets.

'Go on, you blokes,' said Mick. 'I'll catch you up.'

'Wagging class are we, Jamieson?' Masterman's voice boomed across the yard. 'Come here.'

Mick shook his head. 'I'm doing a job, sir. For the history teacher.'

'In the toilets, boy? Get over here at once. Move when I tell you.'

Mick ran to where he stood.

'Now, just what sort of a job are you doing for which history teacher?'

'For the new one, sir. She's got us this period and she's sent us – me and Tom and Danny – to get two buckets of dirt.'

Masterman rocked on his heels. 'You couldn't lie straight in bed, Jamieson. And just what would you be doing with two buckets of dirt, in history of all lessons? Agriculture maybe. Science maybe. But history!' He spat the word out.

The window of Penny's classroom was open. Mick saw her move across the room and stop when she heard Masterman's voice. She saw them talking and leant slowly forward, her elbows on the sill.

'We're making models, sir. Of the olden days. She's over there at the window. You ask her.' He paused. 'I've got to go.'

29

'Any problem?' Penny's cool voice rang out across the quadrangle.

Masterman turned for a moment as if he was going to answer but then shook his head, glanced to where Mick had disappeared behind the trees at the edge of the car park and walked off towards the oval.

'Masterman got me,' said Mick as he watched Tom shovel dirt into the bucket. 'Dickhead. I thought he was going to have a go at her too.'

'Who?'

'The history teacher. She was at the window watching while he raved on.'

'What'd he say?'

'Just the usual.'

They tipped the dirt into the metal tray that Penny had set up across two desks under the window.

'That took you long enough.' She turned to Mick. 'You had a problem, I see.'

He shrugged but didn't reply.

'OK.' She spoke now to the group. 'You've got the dirt. What's the next step?'

'Make the hills.'

'Put the river in.'

'And the road.'

'Mm. Don't you think you should check the maps? You think you know it, but things have changed. The road especially. There wasn't always a freeway, you know. And maybe the river. Those ovals behind the shopping centre used to be a swamp.' She reached across to the next table and picked up a couple of photos. 'See what I mean?

You've only got ten minutes so have a look at these and the maps on the other table. You can get stuck into it tomorrow.'

She left them and went to the group working near the door.

Tom picked up the photographs and began to flick through them.

'You should've seen the look on Masterman's face,' said Mick.

'Shut up about Masterman. You're always going on about him.' Tom dropped a photo on the desk. 'Look, that's where we are. The school. Only it was a cow paddock then.'

The bell was about to go. Penny clapped her hands for quiet and waited while all the books were brought to the front.

'Shh,' she said. 'You can go on with that next time. There's one more thing. At assembly after recess, there's going to be an announcement about a school play. It's a musical actually. We're doing it at the end of second term. Ms Mitchell and I are going to be in charge of it and we have decided – ' She paused and motioned with her hand for Tom to sit down. He had stood up and was inching his way to the door. 'This affects you, Tom. It's a musical about gangs of thieves and robbers. In fact, you're a bit of a gang leader yourself. You'd probably be a natural for one of the parts.'

He put his bag down and sat on the edge of the desk.

'Come on, miss. Me? Act?' He pushed his sleeve up and flexed his muscles.

'Unless we do Crocodile Dundee Three.'

Cheryl and Tammy groaned.

Tom grinned at them and then back at Penny. 'Or we could make a history video. I'll be Ned Kelly.'

'OK. OK, Tom. Settle down.' Penny was grinning too. 'We have decided that every student in the first three years will try out for a part. There's a big chorus. Lots of street kids. Other roles too. You lot don't have a big exam year this year so you're ideal. We need lots of you to audition.'

'Aw, miss. I'm not trying out.'

'You are, Danny Brett. There aren't many occasions when you absolutely have to do something – but this is one of them. You might have one of the best singing voices in the school.'

'Sing! I'm not singing on my own. Not in front of everyone.'

'Tammy'll be in it. She's always in that sort of thing.'

'And Chris. They were in stuff last year.'

Penny shrugged. 'I'm not really interested in who's always in it. I want to see where all the talent is that we don't know about. You can be good at sport and good at singing too, you know. Ms Mitchell will tell you more in your music lesson. You're all going to give it a try. It'll be a lot of fun. And –' she paused and grinned again as the bell sounded ' – there'll probably have to be some time off classes for rehearsal.'

'How old are you, Nan?'

Mick's grandmother looked up from the crossword. The bridge of her glasses was broken and stuck together with a Bandaid. It meant he couldn't see her eyes properly. She peered over the rims at him.

'As old as my tongue and a bit older than my teeth.'

'No. Really.'

'What do you want to know for?'

'History.'

'History? How come all this sudden interest in history? Ask me a question about maths.'

Mick scratched his head and pulled a face. 'What number is your age?'

'OK, OK. Seventy-five. Now why do you want to know?'

'It's like that other stuff we were doing. About us. We're doing the district. We're going to make a model. Everyone said to ask you what it was like.'

'I wasn't around in the convict days, if that's what they want.' She looked back down at the newspaper in front of her.

Mick went on, 'I told you before, it's not convicts. It's just a while ago, before the freeway, before the new houses. Probably when Dad was a kid.'

She took her glasses off then and put them down on top of the paper. 'We moved here in nineteen forty-seven,' she said. 'We built the house around us and it was pretty hard because the war was just over and you couldn't get materials for building. Lees' was the only other one when your grandfather and I built this one. None of that shopping centre was there. There were a couple of shops on Prince Street. And no buses either. You had to walk if you didn't have a car. The old highway was the main road. Your dad used to ride his bike to school. Him and all his mates. They used to play in the creek that ran along the back of the shops. That was before the creek got filled in and they built ovals.'

'What did he used to play?'

His grandmother put her glasses back on and picked up the paper. 'I have no idea. Ask him when he comes through next time.'

Mick lay on the floor of his bedroom, *Truckin' Life, 1988* open in front of him. He couldn't concentrate. He got up and went over to the window. There was no breeze. He picked up the silver trophy from the bookcase at the end of his bed. A miniature football on top of a tall silver shaft. Awarded to his father in his last year of school, the year they beat every other team in the district. He rubbed the silver against his shirt till the black grime from the metal transferred itself to the blue cotton.

He heard his grandmother walking round the house, locking up. He dropped his clothes to the floor, turned out the light and lay down. Through the open window came night sounds, crickets, the calling of voices and car engines. For a while, moonlight, broken by the branches of the lemon tree, shone on the BMX posters on the wall and rested on the silver trophy. But then clouds blew over and the room went dark. Under the sheet, the numbers on his watch glowed, silvery green.

WANTED

ACTORS/SINGERS
for the musical

"OLIVER"

AUDITION TODAY

MUSIC ROOM - LUNCHTIME

ALL WELCOME

NO EXPERIENCE NECESSARY!!!

(LOTS OF PARTS FOR PEOPLE WHO DON'T WANT
TO SING ON THEIR OWN - STREET KIDS,
POLICE, LONDONERS ETC.)

MEMO TO ALL STAFF

<u>Subject:</u>   School Musical.   OLIVER

Auditions for this production are taking place now. All students with the exception of those in year twelve are being encouraged to take part. When decisions have been made, a list of those involved will be circulated to all staff so that it can be checked whenever absences are necessary. Some assistance will be sought from staff, at a later date, for different aspects of the production. The summary below is the one which all players will get and it is included here for your interest.

<u>Story:</u>   The musical OLIVER is based on the novel <u>Oliver Twist</u> by Charles Dickens. The main character, Oliver, is a young boy living in the workhouse. When the play opens, he and the other children are having their meal of gruel. The matron and the beadle are stunned when Oliver asks for more. He is quickly removed from the `home' and taken to a funeral director's where he is to work for his food and lodgings.

Oliver is tormented by another boy who is also employed there and when Oliver fights this boy, the beadle is called and told that he must take Oliver back.

Oliver runs away and is met on the streets by the Artful Dodger. He offers Oliver a place to sleep. In fact, he is recruiting Oliver to become a pickpocket with a gang of boys who roam the streets. The items they steal are taken back to Fagin

– an old man who is their `teacher' and who seems to run the house where they live.

Back at these rooms, Oliver is introduced to Fagin and watches him teaching the boys how to pick his pocket. He also meets **Nancy** an older girl and **Bill** – her boyfriend who is a much more experienced and violent criminal than the others.

The next day, Oliver goes out with the Dodger on his first job. An old man's pocket is picked. Oliver is not responsible but he is the only one of the boys who is caught. He is taken before a magistrate, the truth is revealed by a shopkeeper and Oliver is released into the care of the old man, **Mr Brownlow**. Meanwhile, Dodger reports back to Fagin who fears that Oliver will talk about the boys and reveal the hideout. Nancy is sent to try to bring Oliver back.

Oliver runs a message for Mr Brownlow. Nancy grabs him and and drags him, protesting, back to Fagin. Bill and Fagin are both cruel to Oliver and demand to know whether he has talked about them.

Nancy is sorry for what she has done to Oliver. She agrees to take him to London Bridge and hand him back to Mr Brownlow.

Back at the workhouse, **a dying old woman** confesses that she took a locket from the body of Oliver's dead mother many years before. The beadle takes the locket and sets out to look for Oliver. He eventually arrives at Mr Brownlow's and we discover that the locket contains a picture of Mr Brownlow's daughter. Oliver is his grandson. (Or at least that's how it is in our version!)

In the final scene, Nancy brings Oliver to the bridge. They are pursued by Bill who shoots Nancy, grabs Oliver and runs with him over the rooftops. They are followed by the police. Bill is shot and Oliver is reunited with his grandfather.

Characters.

People are needed to play all the characters in the story summary as well as many more. The kids do not have to be expert singers. There are parts for street kids, police, Londoners, workhouse kids – in other words LOTS.

Talk to everyone in your classes. Tell them it's going to be lots of fun. See if you can get them to come to audition.

<u>NO EXPERIENCE NECESSARY</u> !!!

Four

'OK.' Bella, the music teacher, walked up and down in front of the group on stage. 'Before we start this time let me say a couple of things. In this show, you're street brats. You steal. You live in squalor. In dirt. In filth. Rubbish. You don't have any of the fancy things that you kids take for granted. No television, no comfortable bed with the cover in your favourite cartoon characters.'

She stopped in front of Tom. 'There's no pinball, no videos, no McDonald's. There probably isn't enough to eat and if there is, it'll only be bread and water. Your parents are dead or they've deserted you or else you've run away from them. Life's not easy. But – ' she paused and looked at each student in turn ' – you're lively. You can belt out a song.' She tucked her thumbs into imaginary coat lapels and swaggered across the stage. 'Like this. I want to see you hamming it up.'

Tom and Mick both took her off. Behind her back, they strutted, their thumbs tucked up into their armpits, heads held on the side, hips swaying.

Trisha and Debbie laughed.

The teacher spun round. 'That's great,' she said.

Penny, standing in the doorway, clapped loudly. 'Looks like you do act better than you write history.'

Mick pushed Tom. 'Show us how to do it,' he hissed.

'Show us yourself.' Tom pushed him back.

The group began.

'Consider yourself, our mate,

Consider yourself, one of the family . . . '

'Move around,' said the teacher.

'We've taken to you so strong . . . '

Mick stuck one hand in his pocket. He tucked the other one under his armpit and leaned forward, his head on one side, the way the teacher had. His voice was strong and clear. It was fun. Like swinging out over the river on the knotted vine, burning down Milkshake Hill on his bike, or taking Tom's skateboard up and over the ramp. He wanted to muck around, to laugh. He led the group across the stage, chest out, shoulders swinging. Tom stepped back, his hands loose at his sides.

The song finished. Tom was staring at him.

'Boy, you got a bit carried away! They'll put you in it if you're not careful.'

'No way.' But he wasn't sure.

For the rest of the lesson he sat close under the window. He half listened as Tom whispered something to Danny. Something about the machines in the arcade near the station. They'd be going after school.

Out the front, it was the last group's turn. Tammy grinned as she swung her way across the stage. Her voice carried above the others. Did she feel the same as he had? The rest were barely moving. When they finished, Penny came to the front of the room, and she and the music teacher stood by the piano, talking. Mick thought they were looking at him but when the bell went for recess they said nothing.

Mick ran to catch up to Tom and Danny. They were at the front of the group and had got to the canteen first. He cut across the verandah by the art room and leapt over the rail.

'Jamieson!'

Mick stumbled.

'Jamieson! Come here, boy.'

Mick stopped and turned slowly to face Masterman.

'And where are you off to in such a hurry?'

'The canteen.'

'Is that the way to address a teacher?'

'No, sir.'

'Well, boy, answer my question. And look at me while you're talking.'

'I was going to the canteen,' he paused slightly, 'sir.'

'Right. And is there any need to charge for it like a bull at a gate?'

'The pies get cold . . . sir.'

'That is no reason to leap over the verandah and land in the garden.'

Mick shifted his weight from one foot to the other. The pies would be sold out by now. Penny and the music teacher came through the doorway onto the verandah. They saw him talking to Masterman. Penny put her hand on the other woman's arm and they both stopped.

'I didn't land on the garden . . . sir. I missed . . .'

'Don't be cheeky.'

'But I didn't.'

'Can't you understand plain English? I said don't be cheeky.' The PE teacher rolled forward on the balls of his feet and pressed his finger into Mick's chest. His breath smelt of peppermint lifesavers. 'And if I get any more lip out of you, son, you can come with me and explain yourself to the boss.'

He turned and strode away towards the oval.

Mick stood for a moment. He hadn't landed on the garden. He hadn't done any damage. Masterman knew it too. Stuff you, Masterman. No pies by now. And no Coke either. And Tom and Danny could be anywhere. The bell would probably be going in the next five minutes. His stomach rumbled. He kicked a clod of dirt so it spattered all over the path.

Penny tapped him on the shoulder.

'You know that character we were talking about this morning? The cheeky gang leader. The one who takes on people much bigger than he is?' She and the music teacher were both grinning. 'You're perfect for the part. We want you.'

Mick sat on the footpath on the bridge over the freeway. His back pressed against the metal railings. There was no one else in sight.

They'll put you in it if you're not careful.

Why had he let the music get to him? Why hadn't he stayed cool? Like Tom. Like Dad. He always got what he wanted.

You're perfect for the part. We want you.

Heads I do it. Tails I don't.

He held a coin in the palm of his hand. It was cold. Tom and Danny would be up at the arcade. They never asked him any more. In year six they'd take their bikes and skateboards and hang around the roads where they were building the new houses, but not now. They both got heaps of pocket money. 'If you want pocket money,' Nan said, 'you've got to earn it. And I can only give you a couple of dollars. Ask your father when he comes back next time.'

Mick rubbed the rough edge of the coin. Heads I do it. Tails I don't. He closed his fist. But I don't want to. Everyone staring and you have to learn all those lines and if you forget one . . . He swung around and put his feet through the rails so that they hung out over the road. He closed his eyes and felt again the rush that had come over him when he was on stage. It started somewhere in his stomach and spread till it caught his throat and his whole body tingled.

And if I do, Dad might come. Nan would for sure.

He noticed a Kenworth with three new white vans on the top deck coming towards him. They swayed and bounced, their chains almost invisible. What if they fell? Twisted metal. Smashed glass. Only fools lose their load, Dad said. What else did he say? Only fools work inside, nine to five. Give me the road, any day. That's me.

Mick gripped the rails and squeezed them till the hard metal ridges almost cut his skin. Then he held up the coin again.

Heads I do it. Tails I don't.

Heads he comes home this weekend. Tails he doesn't.

He flipped the coin high in the air and watched as it spun up and out over the rail and down onto the freeway below.

*

In the kitchen of the old house. Mick watches his father heat cold chicken from the night before. Outside it is raining, hard, driving rain, and the noise of it on the roof almost drowns out his words.

'I've been driving trucks for fifteen years. I can't earn a living any other way. And there isn't the work in town. That's why you can't stay with me up here. I can't live down there with Nan and with you but I'll come when I can, every few weeks with a bit of luck. I'll just turn up when I get a load going south to Sydney. I probably won't write first. I'm not much good at writing letters. I'll ring if I get a chance. It won't be too different.' He stood by the stove, his hands loose at his sides, sweat on his forehead. 'I know Nan is not the same as Mum and me. But then I used to be away a lot then too. And Nan loves you and she's getting on a bit. It'll be good for her to have you. You'll be OK. We'll get your bag packed tonight and tomorrow we'll be off.'

Mick says nothing.

Sunday night

Dear Fran:

Note the new address. I've just spent the
weekend unpacking my boxes and suitcases.
Who'd have thought one person could
accumulate so much junk. Bella has retired
to her room and her violin to play for a
while. So far we're getting on well. We seem
to have fairly similar views on lots of
things.

Have spent the last week moving and on
top of that there's this musical. We've been
casting the principals and one of the
amazing things was that we cast that kid
Mick in one of the roles. It was Bella's idea
at first. He can certainly sing and we're
confident that he can act. It'll be a great
way of involving him in school life. I
watch him in class sometimes, and I see him
as one of those immature kids who's got to
prove himself to kids who are a bit older
and a bit more established in groups or in
friendships. Some of them are up to
shaving and getting a bit serious with the
girls and he's still into mucking around
like a little kid. They often can't be
bothered with him. The responsibility of

being in the play could be really good for him. Make him grow up a bit.

When I think about him and about other kids who are a bit like him, I'm reminded of all those hours spent at college discussing child psychology and educational philosophy. It's not theory anymore. It's screwed up kids' lives. I sometimes worry that I've hardly got a clue what to do.

We haven't announced all our plans to the staff yet. I imagine there'll be some who see the show as a time waster. The boss is supportive though, so that should help. You sound very happy in your letters. I get the feeling that you're on top of the teaching and really settled into life on the coast. Remember we used to say we'd teach for a year and then travel? Sounds like we're both too busy to think about it!

I'm off to bed. I've got assignments to mark but they'll have to wait till morning.

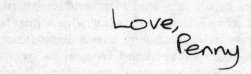

Love,
Penny

Five

'I'm not doing it.'

Mick stood on the low stage in the music room, his arms folded across his chest. 'You can't make me.'

'We're not trying to make you do anything,' said Penny. She was standing in the middle of the room, among the chairs. 'We just think that you're right for this part. You know what we're looking for – cheeky, cocky kid, someone who'll stand up to Fagin. It's a perfect description of you.' She looked across at Bella, who was leaning against the piano. 'Like we said on Friday – you've got an excellent voice, good strong pitch, you can act.'

'No.'

'Why not?'

Mick didn't answer. He pushed his hands down into the pockets of his shorts and looked at the floor.

'Come on. Come down here.' She sat and patted the chair beside her. Like Nan's voice on the nights when they sat up till late and Dad still didn't come.

Mick came slowly off the stage and sat down a few chairs away. Bella stayed by the piano.

'You don't have to be nervous about it. You'll be well prepared. There's no time when you'd be on the stage all by yourself. You do sing a bit on your own but there's always a chorus for the others to join in.'

'I'm not nervous.' He tapped the base of his chair and still didn't look at her. 'I just don't want to.'

From the piano Bella said, 'We'll have loads of fun. And on the big night you can have all your family come and watch.'

Penny interrupted quickly. 'This is the sort of thing you'll remember about school, Mick. You'll forget most of the teachers and probably most of the stuff that you learn . . . '

'So why bother coming?'

'That's not the point.'

In the background, Bella started to play. It wasn't the loud music that they sang to in class. It was softer, quieter, the sort of music that runs round in your head and you know it without ever remembering when you first heard it.

'I watched you Friday,' said Penny. 'You were really enjoying yourself. This could be the biggest, the most important thing you do in your whole school career.'

Mick looked up at her. How could she know what it felt like? What else did she know?

'It's going to be a grand production – even get your photo into the local paper. You'll have all the staff behind you. The principal is keen.'

All the staff? Masterman?

'Is it the others? Are you worried about what Tom and Danny and your mates'll say?'

'They aren't my mates.'

Bella stopped playing.

Penny stood up. 'Think about it some more and tell us Monday. Just don't decide on the basis of what the others think. You work out what you want.

We're going to have a lot of fun. Come and see me at lunchtime. We really want you – but you have to be prepared to work. You'll get taken out of lessons a lot towards the end.' She raised an eyebrow. 'I might even be able to get you off PE lessons!'

Mick lined up the eight ice-block sticks that were the front of his model pub. He spread the glue over the frame and began to fix each one to it. That made two rooms. He leant over to take extra sticks from Chris's pile.

'Get out,' said Chris. 'They're mine. Get your own.'

Mick went over to the box where the modelling materials were kept.

Do it. Don't do it. Do it. Don't do it.

There were no sticks left. He came back to his desk where Debbie was making a set of shepherd's huts.

'Give us your spare sticks, Deb.'

She put her hand over the few she had left.

'Get away.'

Penny looked up from where she was bent over Tammy's work. 'What's the matter, Mick?'

'Nothing. I just need some more sticks and no one'll give 'em to me.'

'Well, you'll just have to make do with what you've got.'

'But I can't do it without them. It won't work.'

She came over to where he was sitting. 'Go out to the trees near the verandah and get some twigs. They'll look better than these sticks anyway. If anyone stops you, tell them to speak to me.'

He left the room.

Get out of PE lessons. Get out of history too.

When he got back, Chris had fixed the verandah to the general store and pushed his chair back. He squinted at the model and let the chair fall forward. The verandah was on a lean.

'D'you reckon it's crooked?' he asked Mick.

'What? Um, yeah. Doesn't matter. The real one's crooked too.'

Reasons for: They want me to.

Reasons against: They want me to.

Reasons for: Because I'll get off school. Nan might come and think it's great.

Dad might come.

Reasons against: Tom and Danny'll think I'm a crawler. Only crawlers do stuff like that.

Mick looked across at Tom. He was sticking photographs of the district over the last hundred years on a huge sheet of cardboard. Trisha and Ariana were cutting them out too and pasting them so they overlapped. A collage, Penny called it. She got really keen when Trisha suggested it.

'It can go up on the wall,' she said. 'Over the model.'

Tom wanted to help them. 'Models are kids' stuff.'

But really he wanted to work with Trisha. As Mick watched, Tom said something to her and she laughed loudly. Beside them, Quoc was doing the headings in huge, careful black letters.

Reasons for: Especially good to get out of PE. Really good to bug Masterman.

50

Reasons against: If I forgot lines or anything I'd feel really stupid. Tom and Danny aren't in it. But then they play cricket on Saturday morning and I don't do that. And they'll go in Masterman's precious football team.

The front of the pub was finished. He started on the side walls. His last six sticks and the glue again. The tops of his fingers were covered in its thin coating. He scratched at it and peeled it off. Tom hadn't been over since school had started. He hadn't been over much in the holidays either. Just once to fix the puncture in his bike and once when they went off to Wollongong for the day to see his brother. Tom had asked Danny first but he couldn't go for some reason.

. . . Photo in the paper.

Do it to nark Tom.

He pushed the glue across to Chris. The scissors and the book they were copying from fell onto the floor. Penny looked up, startled.

'Don't worry, miss. Just Mick chucking his stuff around,' said Tom and he and Trisha laughed together.

'Shut up,' Mick yelled.

'Quiet, the pair of you.' Penny stood up and frowned.

'You don't have to follow Tom,' Nan had said when Mick told her about the play. 'Think for yourself for a change. The play'll be fun.'

'D'you reckon Dad might come?'

'He might. We could try and arrange it. If he

knows far enough in advance he might get a run to Sydney about then.' And she told Mick about a musical show she had been in during the war, raising money for the Red Cross. 'I did a tap dance,' she said and she danced for him in the kitchen, slowly, holding up her skirt and clicking her heavy black shoes on the faded lino. 'You must get your talent from me. Your father couldn't sing to save himself.'

'It might have come from my mother.'

'True. It might.'

Sometimes, in bed at night or walking home in brilliant sunshine, he squeezed his eyes shut tight as possible and tried to remember his mother's face. All that came was the image in the photographs. The wedding one that Nan kept in tissue paper in the bottom drawer, Dad in black suit, Mum with confetti in her hair, and a smaller one with a dog-eared corner that Dad had given him. 'You have this,' he'd said. 'I've got others.' It was taken at the beach. She was thin but suntanned, shielding her eyes. The two had been taken seven years apart and were so different that Mick struggled to find the real face in between. 'What was she like?' he wanted to ask Dad when he did come and they sat after tea in the kitchen. Would she have been pleased?

Do it to please Nan, please Dad.

Please.

But if he doesn't come . . .

He glued the walls to the frame. The pub had a hole at the front for a door and two side holes, higher up, for windows. Tom, Trisha and Ariana finished their collage. Quoc stuck the heading across the top.

Penny clapped her hands for silence.

'Look, everyone. This is our main heading. We'll put the poster over the display. Over here in the corner of the room.'

She waved her hand to take in the finished model of the local area. The metal tray now had a couple of hills and the river valley. Three houses were already pressed down into the dirt.

'Watch it,' she said to Tom as he brushed past the tray and moved to sit next to Mick. 'We don't want any of this stuff knocked over. It'd make a helluva mess. The cleaners'd never forgive us.'

Mick turned and she caught his eye. 'Don't forget. Lunchtime Monday.'

Tom turned to him. 'What you doing with her? You're not going in that stupid play, are you?'

Mick pushed his model to the centre of the desk and rolled up the newspaper. 'I just might,' he said.

Fran,
Thought I'd send you
this to remind you of
Old haunts. Came in with
the senior English classes
to see a production of
Othello. Superb! Makes
our attempt seem so
amateurish. Have to
start somewhere!
Find out Monday if
Mick's going to do it.
Seems really important
to me that he
does!
      Penny

POST CARD

Six

Mick knocked on the door of the English staffroom. No answer. He leant back on the verandah post for a moment and then knocked again. He pushed the door open and looked in. The room was empty. Books were scattered over desks and on chairs. They were piled up on the floor, on top of cupboards and on the radiator. Stale coffee smell.

'What are you doing, Jamieson? That area's out of bounds at lunchtime.'

Mr White, on playground duty, stood under the straggly bottlebrush in the middle of the lower playground and his voice echoed off the buildings.

Mick quickly shut the door. He stepped back onto the verandah as the geography teacher came towards him, shielding his red face from the sun.

'Looking for someone, sir.' Mick looked up and squinted.

'What've you done this time?'

'Nothing.'

'Nothing who?'

'Nothing, sir.'

'Well, then. Who are you looking for?' Mr White waved for him to come down. 'Come on, son. I can't wait here all day talking to you.'

'The new history teacher, sir.' He stopped himself from saying Penny. 'It's about the play.'

'The play. What play?'

'With music and singing. She's doing it. And the music teacher.'

'Oh, yes.' There was a pause for a minute. 'It's Miss Lane you want. Though I don't know why she'd want you. She's at a meeting. Wait for her near the common room. And don't make any noise outside the door.'

Mick followed the path that led across the front of the tuckshop and around to the library block and the administration. Tom was coming down the steps.

'Where've you been?' said Mick.

'Where you going yourself?'

Mick didn't answer.

Tom suddenly grinned. 'You're going to see her about that play. You're going to do it, aren't you?'

'What if I am?'

Tom laughed. 'You're not gunna, are you?'

Mick looked away from him and rubbed the toe of his shoe against the face of the step. 'They want me to. I'm just going to try it. See what it's like.'

'What a laugh. What are ya?' Tom laughed again, jumped off the step onto the grass and ran towards the oval.

Mick looked across the hall to the open door of the common room. The whole staff was there. Teachers sat on the chairs, on the tables and leant against the walls. Mrs Pine stood like she did at assembly, waving a bunch of papers in one hand.

'. . . That's all I've got to say. I'm going to hand you over to one of the newer members of staff. Penny from history and Bella from music are going ahead with their idea of doing a school musical. I've said OK to their plans. It's a few years since we've done anything quite on this scale here.' She took her glasses off and sucked the end of them.

Mick moved quickly across the hall and stood beside the open door where no one inside could see him.

'Anyway, I want to give them all the support they need. There'll be lots of jobs for everyone before they're through. I know we are all overworked . . .' There was a low murmur when she said that. '. . . but it's a wonderful opportunity for everyone to be involved. Let's make it a real communal effort.'

Her chair scraped as she sat down. Papers rustled. Mick heard Penny's voice but couldn't see her.

'This list I'm passing round is the cast. The first half are the main ones. That big group at the end are really like a chorus. The principals start rehearsal next week. We don't imagine there will be too much disruption at first. We'll use lunchtimes and after school and we'll be in the music room, not in the main hall. We have to be honest, though. As we get closer to the final stages, we'll probably cut into a few lessons and we'll be calling on people to give us a hand.'

Bella interrupted. 'Anyone who wants to volunteer to help right now – in any way – we'd really appreciate it. Especially if you've ever done this sort of thing before.'

'I've done some stage managing,' said Mick's English teacher, Mr Richards.

'Need any singers?' Mick didn't recognize that voice. 'At my school, the staff took part as well.'

'No, thanks.' That was the music teacher again. 'No offence but there's enough talent among the kids. We've found a few beauties. You'll be surprised.'

There was silence for a moment. Mick moved into the shadow of the corridor. He could see Mr Stanley from the industrial arts class reading the sheets of paper. Behind him was a new maths teacher whose name he didn't know and next to him was Masterman, who was fidgeting. He had stopped reading his papers and turned to speak to whoever was on the other side of him. He cleared his throat and held the papers out in front of him.

'This list,' he said. 'I see you've got young Jamieson on it.'

'Yes.' Penny's voice sounded strange.

'Well, you said I'd be surprised and you're right. I reckon you're crazy.' He pushed his chair back and stood up, shaking the list out in front of him. He rocked forwards and back on the balls of his feet, the way he did when he talked at Mick about forgotten PE shorts.

Mick moved closer to the door. Opposite him was a huge cabinet. In it were small plaster models and pieces of jewellery. The mirror at the back reflected the staff room. Between bits of art work, he could see Penny standing in front of the row of chairs.

'That boy's a ratbag. I wouldn't have him on any team of mine.' Masterman slapped the paper with the flat of his hand.

Someone murmured, 'Hear, hear.'

'It's a play, not a football match.' That was the music teacher.

'He never brings his gear. He's cheeky. He backchats. He's an insolent young lout. In this sort of thing – we want kids this school can be proud of. A boy like this'll just let you down.' His voice grew louder and he moved out of Mick's sight, into the middle of the room. 'I know it's your show and you think you know what you're doing but I had run-ins with him last year. That boy is a bludger.'

Mick clenched his fists. He took short sharp breaths.

Don't let me down now, Mick. I know you're only a bit of a kid, but while I'm gone you're the man of the house. It's up to you to look after Mum. You do everything she wants you to while I'm up north.

'Come on, Masterman.' Mr Richards spoke up. 'That's a bit strong. I've got the boy for English and I don't have any trouble from him. He's no saint, but show me a kid who is.'

'He's a liar. He's no good. He'll leave you in the lurch at the last moment when it's too late to get someone else to do it.'

Don't let me down.

Mick stepped out of the shadow.

'He might be able to sing a bit but mark my words, you can't trust him. I've said it before and I'll say it again, a boy like that will only let you down.'

Mick was in the doorway. He looked from Masterman to Penny. She saw him and jumped to her feet.

Mick ran. He pushed past the principal's secretary, who was coming through the main door. He almost fell the six steps to the ground, caught his balance and headed along the path to the back playground.

Tom and Danny were at the edge of the oval,

59

coming towards him. Quick. Run. They hadn't seen him yet. He ducked off the path towards the steps of the history classroom. He charged through a game of handball.

'Watch it!'

The tennis ball hit him on the thigh. He knocked it away into another group of kids, leapt over a couple of bags and landed heavily, twisting his ankle. Shit! He hauled himself up by the rail on the steps leading to the history room, pushed the door open with his shoulder and fell against the first desk. He caught his breath and then thumped the wooden desk top hard with his closed fist. The skin on his knuckles split. Blood spurted from the back of his hand. He leapt up and lifted the desk high above his head and hurled it towards the far wall. It landed on the project table. The metal tray crashed to the floor. Mud and water flew in the air, spattered on the windows, splashed over the walls and the charts. Papier-mâché and plywood structures shattered and fell into a heap. Mick picked up a chair and smashed it down hard onto the table. He kicked and kicked at the mess on the floor. Pieces flew in all directions.

He staggered back against the teacher's desk.

His breathing slowed. He felt his way around the corner of the table and slumped into Penny's chair.

The room was quiet and still.

At his feet were the splintered remains of his model pub.

He knelt and started to pick them up.

The door behind him opened. He turned and saw Penny standing there, her white knuckles gripping the door handle, her face twisted, her mouth open.

Home,
Monday night

Dear Fran:

I've just got to sit down and write to
someone. Bella's gone out to a meeting.
There's no one around here I can let it all
out onto. You're it. I have had enough of
work and stupid people.

First of all, Masterman. Remember the
Neanderthal? He has objected to my casting
of that boy, Mick, in the play. His reasons?
He says that Mick is a liar, a ratbag and
will only let me down.

It's not bad enough that he announces this
in the staff meeting, but the boy is waiting
outside, because I had told him to come and
see me. Of course he hears everything, goes
off his brain, races out of the building and
ends up in my history room, smashing the
place up.

I'm not excusing him - I nearly died when I
saw what he'd done - but then just as I
was about to start into him, he shrivelled
up as if he realized that he was behaving
in exactly the way that Masterman said he
would.

I don't know, Fran. This kid has become the

most amazing challenge for me. It started
out that he was just a bit screwed up and I
thought that by taking a bit of a special
interest in him, I could help. It seems that
now I have to be his champion. I hardly
know him, but what can I do? I could just
say O.K. Get lost. Wash my hands of the
whole thing. Drop him from the play. But if
I do that, aren't I over-reacting to one
mistake? Showing that I don't understand
how he felt?

What he overheard today was really
devastating. I don't know what I'd've done
if it were me.

If I desert him, I'm saying that I don't
believe in the power of people to learn
something from their behaviour and to grow
up and change. And I do believe that.
That's all part of wanting to be a teacher
in the first place. Isn't it?

Maybe Masterman is right. Maybe the kid
is a liar and he can't be depended on.
He would have this kid expelled. He
thinks we should bring back caning and
this is exactly the sort of case where
he'd use it.

But things like the play are not just
rewards you hand out for good behaviour. I
feel like taking a risk with Mick.

This afternoon, after it was all over, I was sitting in the history room. It was all cleaned up. I was feeling really low and Gordon Richards came in and we talked for about half an hour. He says it's up to me what I do but I'm fairly sure that he'll support me if I argue for keeping Mick on. And that he'd be disappointed if I did otherwise. That would be consistent with the thoughtful, gentle way he handles people and problems. He really likes kids and most of them like him.

Sorry to bore you with all this. I guess I never thought it would be this hard. I knew about the marking and the preparation, the time-consuming stuff. But no one tells you about the moral dilemmas! And I think the clashes between staff are the worst bit.

Too many more days like this one and I'll be lucky to finish the year. By the sound of your last letter, things aren't all as rosy for you as they seemed at first. Want to join me in an escape to somewhere exotic? Paris? Rome? Rio?

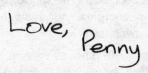

Love, Penny

Report on the incident which took place in Room 13a, Monday. 19th March 1990.

To: The Principal.
The Head of the Department of History

On Monday 19th March, certain items of furniture were damaged in Rm 13a. The student involved, Michael Jamieson, had overheard extremely negative comments about him being expressed by a member of staff at the weekly staff meeting. He went to the room where he proceeded to damage some of the furniture. Two tables and one chair are beyond repair. At the same time, I regret to add, certain student work was also destroyed. The boy has undertaken to spend an hour before school, for as long as necessary, restoring this student work. He will also spend time on this task tomorrow instead of attending the year eight excursion.

While not wishing to condone the boy's actions in any way, I do feel that the comments he overheard must have distressed him in such a way as to arouse considerable anger and frustration. I do not think that any useful purpose would be gained by further disciplinary action such as banning him from the school play. He should be encouraged to channel his energies, not have his already poor self – image reinforced.

Penny Lane
HISTORY

Seven

Mick was late. He stood beside the gate into the teachers' car park and waited as year eight broke away from the assembly and headed for the coaches parked out the front. Tom was at the back, laughing at something with Danny. He punched him in the shoulder, in a friendly way, and Danny tossed his bag in the air, caught it and swung it out wide behind him. In front of them, Trisha slowed down so that the other girls reached the coaches first and she was the last to get on.

Mick watched as Tom and Danny joined her on the back seat. She turned to look out of the window. She pointed at Mick and said something so that Tom turned round, and, as the coach started, fell sideways against her, one hand towards Mick, fingers sticking upwards.

Mick stood in the open doorway. Quoc's sign, the only thing untouched by the mess, still hung over the empty space where the model had been. The room was quiet. Clean. No mud, no sand, none of the water that had been spattered over everything the day before.

Penny stood behind her table. On three desks pushed together she had spread newspaper, sticks, glue and paint.

'Morning,' she said, raising one eyebrow. 'I thought maybe you weren't coming.'

Mick didn't reply.

'What did your grandmother say when you told her?'

Mick shrugged. 'She . . . she reckons if Dad was here he'd've belted the daylights out of me.' He looked at the floor. It was dry but stained where the mud had seeped into the grain.

Penny raised the eyebrow again.

'I'm not going to stay long,' she said. 'I've got some marking and other classes to get ready. I've put out all the stuff you'll need. Get as much done as you can. At least there are no distractions.' She shuffled papers on the table for a few minutes.

Mick dropped his bag and sat down.

'See you at recess,' she said.

He worked slowly at first, sorting out the sticks for the different models. 'You have to rebuild the lot,' Penny had said. 'I've told the staff and I've told the kids that the whole model will be reconstructed as quickly as possible. You are to miss excursions, recess and lunch breaks. I don't think there'll be any trouble.' She had taken the class to another room and left him to clean the mess. When he had finished, she had sent him home so that he wouldn't have to face the others.

Two pubs. Five shops. A school. A church. Houses. It'd take days.

His hands shook as he laid out the frame.

They'd be almost in the city by now. First stop Darling Harbour and then the Maritime Museum.

Tom sucking up to Trisha. Danny on with someone too. What had they all said when Penny told them? He didn't want to ask. But he wanted to know. Tom, Danny, Trisha. Even Chris and Quoc. They'd hate him. Never talk to him. Or worse. Head down the toilet. Arm twisted and face pushed into the concrete.

It'd happened so quickly. He couldn't remember how he had got into the room. Just the feelings. Smash. Crash. Blood on his knuckles. Cold, shivering, sweat.

He finished the first house quickly.

He took another handful of sticks and carefully added a second room to the building in front of him. The join was crooked and he sat holding the pieces firmly together while the glue set.

'You're in this play, now,' Penny had said. 'I've stuck my neck out for you and I'm damned if I'm going to get my head chopped off. You will rebuild that model and you will be the Artful Dodger and you will do a damned good job or I shall personally tear you limb from limb.'

For a long time he worked quietly, making the frames, laying out the wider sticks for the walls and then gluing them carefully in place. He finished the pub and a second house before the bell rang for the next period. Voices sounded in the corridor outside. Doors opened and closed. He sorted the materials for the department store and then pushed his chair back for a break. He heard Masterman's whistle, loud and piercing from out on the oval. A truck ground its gears as it crept up the hill. Mick looked up. From out near the fence he'd know its make and speed, even guess the load. This morning he didn't even leave his seat.

The bell rang for morning recess. Penny came, bringing a steaming cup of coffee and a can of orange drink.

'Are you ready for this?' She sat down opposite him and blew on the hot coffee for a moment while he drank quietly. He didn't look at her. Then she swung her chair round and looked at the buildings that he had finished and put on the next table.

'You've done a fair bit already,' she said.

He made a vague noise in reply.

'Pity the class wasn't away for a couple of days. Then you'd be finished and we could get straight back to normal.' She turned to face him.

Normal. He wouldn't look at her. Smash up the work of the whole class. Wreck everything. He shivered.

'Are you all right?' said Penny.

'Yeah. I'm OK.'

'If you want to talk about it, I'm a good listener.'

'Nothing to say.'

She finished her coffee and stood up. 'Work through till lunchtime,' she said. 'Then I've got another idea. Some of the main actors in the play are having a meeting. The older kids, I mean. I think you should come along and get to know them a bit. You're going to have to work with them quite a lot in the next few months.'

By the time the bell went for lunch, Mick had

finished three houses, one of the pubs and the department store. He had done the frame for the church and was just lining up the sticks for the walls when Penny came back and stopped him.

'You've done enough for one day. Take that stuff home and work on it tonight. I want you to put your mind on the play for the rest of the afternoon.'

In the music room there were plates of sandwiches, cups of juice and a cake. Half a dozen kids from years ten and eleven were sitting around on the carpet, eating and talking to each other. They didn't notice Penny and Mick in the doorway.

Mick hesitated. Opposite him was Mark Donovan, who drove his own car to school and at weekends worked in the sports shop in the arcade. At the athletics carnival he had outrun Masterman. Tom reckoned he'd seen him knock a bloke's teeth out in a fight outside the Liverpool pub one Sunday afternoon. His mate with the long fair hair tied back was also there.

Penny whispered, 'Get yourself a drink and then come over here.' She went and stood next to the piano.

'Excuse me, everyone,' she said, 'we thought this was a good chance for all of you main characters,' she raised her eyebrows, 'to get to know each other a bit and talk about how we are going to run this show. Make yourself comfortable. Have a drink and a sandwich and then I'll explain who we all are and what we're doing.' She moved over towards Bella, who was standing under the window talking to Margie McGuire.

Mick knew the face. She was school swimming champion. She was in some of the other sports teams as well and was always up on assembly getting trophies. He didn't know she could sing. She wouldn't know him. He looked down at his sandwich.

Penny tapped him on the shoulder and said to the group:

'OK. Introductions first. Youth before age. This is Mick from year eight. He's the Artful Dodger, the cheeky street kid. His singing is great and we think he's the perfect person for the job.' Mick felt his face burn. 'He's not the only year eight person in the show. Tammy Camino isn't here because she's on an excursion and of course there's David in year seven, who is to play Oliver.'

Mick looked up, briefly. A couple of the others nodded.

Penny went on, 'Margie, as most of you know, is our leading lady. She's Nancy who has a heart of gold and comes to a tragic end.'

Margie laughed and raised her cup. 'Here's to tragic heroines,' she said.

'And Mark, over here,' Penny went on, 'is Bill Sykes. He's Nancy's boyfriend, and in the end, he does her in.'

'The brute,' hissed Margie.

Mark flexed his muscles, put his hands around Margie's neck and pretended to strangle her. She rolled her eyes and laughed and fell against him.

When everyone had been spoken about, Penny and Bella moved to the centre of the room and waved them all to sit in a large circle. Mick was between Penny and Margie. He brushed against the girl as he moved into a comfortable position.

'Sorry,' he mumbled and didn't look at her.

'That's OK.'

He held his cup with both hands and stared at the floor as he drank. There was a loose thread sticking out near his right heel, a white thread in a carpet that was dark blue. It didn't make sense.

Penny spoke to them about the staff meeting.

'As usual,' she said, 'there are a few people who think that something like this is a waste of time.'

There were murmuring noises from the group.

'So I don't have to tell you how important it is that we do this really well. Now you lot who are in year eleven have big exams in less than two years. You cannot give anyone any reason to say that they think you're getting slack with your schoolwork. No missed homework. No late assignments.' She looked slowly around the group, finishing with Mick. 'No falling asleep in class and saying you were up all night learning lines.'

Brooke, sitting next to Margie, laughed. They all grinned.

'This applies to you too, Mick. Even though you aren't in an important exam year. Don't let me ever hear the excuse that you couldn't do some work because the play interfered.' Penny grinned.

'Even if it's true?' asked Mick.

'Even if it's true.'

'OK. Now we're going to spend the rest of the session talking about the play itself, something about the characters that you all play and how you see them. We'll make two groups. Bella is going to lead one, I'll lead the other.' She nudged Mick. 'You go off into Bella's group with Margie and Mark. You must be sick of me all the time.'

She turned away quickly and for a moment he was left alone. Margie was leaning forward, talking to Mark, and Bella was organizing some notes in a pile on the carpet in front of her.

Mark's friend Alan sat cross-legged, laughing at something Brooke had said.

Mick couldn't move.

They all belonged. Go now. Say no. They knew each other. They'd done this before. Forget the feeling on stage, the rush. They were seventeen, drove cars, had money. No one yelled at them. No one said they were bludgers. They could leave school if they wanted to.

He felt Margie's hand on his shoulder. She was looking across at Mark but he shrugged his shoulders and shook his head. 'Come on,' she said to Mick, 'we're hopeless. What did Penny say your name was?'

Eight

'Let's start,' said Bella, 'by talking a bit about the sort of people you are.' She nodded to the tall fair-haired boy with the ponytail. 'What about you, Alan? Tell us about Fagin.'

Alan sat up and crossed his legs. 'I'm a crook,' he said. 'I've got all these kids that I've tricked or kidnapped and they live at my place and every day they go out and steal stuff and we live off the money it makes.' He pointed at Mick. 'Dodger over here does the dirty work for me – he keeps everyone in line and makes sure they pinch plenty of stuff and they don't get caught.' Mick looked up. Alan winked at him and gave him the thumbs up, before going on, 'I feed the kids just enough so they don't starve and I keep all the rest for myself.' He grinned. He was used to everyone looking at him. He played lead guitar in the school rock band. He was the tallest kid in the school. Taller than most of the teachers too.

'Anything to add to that, Mick?' asked the teacher.

He scratched at a hole that was starting at the side of his shoe. 'Like he said,' Mick nodded to Alan, 'I'll do what he says and make them get stuff and not get caught. And be the leader when we're singing back where we live, at his – Fagin's place.' He looked up at Alan but he was whispering something to the girl next to him and didn't notice.

Mick looked around the room while the others kept talking. Penny and her group were sitting close together. She was speaking quickly, moving her hands a lot and when she stopped, they all laughed loudly.

He turned back. It was Margie's turn. 'I'm in love with Bill,' she said, waving her hand at Mark, 'or at least I am when I'm Nancy, but he's rotten to me and I like to have a good time too and sometimes I muck around with my mate Dodger.' She grinned at Mick and he found himself grinning back at her.

The excursion coach still wasn't back when Mick walked round to the bus bays at the front of the school. He didn't want to see anyone. He didn't know what he would say to any of them. He rode the bus home in silence, standing in the centre aisle and ignoring seats that became vacant. He didn't head up over the freeway but walked quickly through the streets. Nan wasn't in. He went straight to his room, tipped the model parts over the floor and began to work.

He didn't come out when he heard Nan opening the front door.

'Are you home, Mick?' she called.

'Yeah.' He kept gluing the sticks to the frame of the second pub.

After tea he went back to his room. There were four more buildings to make. He laid the sticks out and began with one of the shops. It was the one Chris had made. Two lopsided verandahs around

74

the single room. When Nan turned the TV off and went to bed, he had almost finished.

She put her head around the door. 'You'd better get some sleep.'

'Won't be long,' he said.

The next morning he put the six finished pieces in a box with bits of newspaper to protect them and caught the early bus. He was sitting outside the English staffroom when Penny arrived.

'Mick!' she said. 'I thought you'd still be in bed at this hour.' She went down to the history room with him and watched while he set the buildings into the fresh tray of soil.

'You can hardly tell the difference,' she said. 'What made you do it all last night? I thought you were going to take days.'

Mick shrugged.

She looked at him closely. 'Was it so you'd be free to learn your lines? Or are you scared that Tom and the others were going to thump you?'

'Bit of both,' said Mick.

'You surprise me,' she said and shook her head. 'And in fact, I've got a surprise for you.' She went to the cupboard at the back of the room. 'I came in after my meeting yesterday and made this.' She took out a huge collage to replace the one that Tom and Trisha had made. The photos were almost the same. 'I thought it would be good to have this back up today.'

Mick stood and watched as she pinned it under Quoc's lettering. His hands were shaking slightly. 'Thanks, miss,' he mumbled.

*

At the end of English, Mr Richards kept Mick back to help carry the box of books that he'd brought down for reading. Tom and Danny left the room slowly, glancing over their shoulders, but when they saw Mick walking with the teacher, they ran ahead to catch up with Trisha.

'How's the play going?' Mr Richards said as they walked towards the staffroom.

'OK,' said Mick.

'Good luck with it then. I'll be working with you in a week or so.'

Mick put the books on the spare table. He waited for Mr Richards to say something about the history room. But he didn't. He just picked up his notes for the next class.

'Get a move on. Science, isn't it? You don't want to be late.'

Mick almost ran from science to history. He didn't want to be stuck in the corridor, Tom in front of him, Danny behind him. He was first into the room. Where to sit? Trapped in the back corner? Up the front near Penny?

Tom pushed him from behind. Mick threw an arm out to save himself and staggered against a chair. It fell and he went with it, his bag slapping against his head as he hit the floor. Other kids filled the room.

'What'cha doing down there, Jamieson?' said Trisha. 'You want to be careful. Might do some damage. Wouldn't want to break anything, would you?'

Tom said nothing, just turned and went to his seat

76

at the back. Danny and Trisha went with him. Chris headed for the window. By the time Mick had stood up and picked up the folder that had fallen from his bag, almost all the desks were taken.

Penny was at the front now and waved him silently to a spare seat at the side. She clapped her hands for quiet.

'OK, everyone. The model is back the way it was last week, but we are not going to do anything more on it just yet.' She spoke quickly as if she were afraid of being interrupted. 'Instead I want you in pairs or groups of three.' She waved her hand. 'Come on, I've got a different activity for you. I'll tell you what it is when you are ready.'

Mick glanced over his shoulder. Groups were forming easily. No one looked at him in a way that meant he could join them.

Penny touched him on the shoulder. 'Come and make a three with Tammy and Cheryl.'

Mick watched Tom from the corner of his eye. He and Trisha were studying a piece of paper, heads bent, shoulders brushing. What did Tom care all of a sudden? He'd smashed stuff often enough, written on the toilet walls, and got sent home from the excursion in year seven. And what would he do? Bashing in the playground? Trip on the stairs? Beating up in the back corridor? He was bigger and he had mates. Who would help? Play practice wasn't every lunchtime . . . recess . . . after school. Sooner or later . . .

Penny clapped her hands. 'The bell is about to go. We'll finish tomorrow.' She stood beside Mick's desk. 'Why don't you stay back and help me?

There's something on the model needs straightening.'

Eight of them sat on the edge of the stage. Penny was in front of them. She had kicked off her shoes, rolled up the bottoms of her jeans and was standing with her hands on her hips.

'You are the main actors,' she said. 'True, everyone on stage has to act, but you're the ones that the audience is watching.'

'No way,' said Mark. 'They only come to watch their own kid.'

'That may be why they come,' said Bella. 'But once they are here, they'll get into the story and it's you lot that they'll be watching.'

'So,' Penny clapped her hands, 'we're going to do some floor exercises to relax you, to get you into your parts. We'll be doing these a lot so try to get used to them quickly.' She beckoned them down off the stage. 'Just stand loosely, relax. Flop your arms. Come on, Mick. Don't crowd David. Give him a bit of room. Let your head drop. Close your eyes. Breathe deeply.' She let her own head fall forward and her voice slowed. 'And again . . . deep breaths.' She let air out with a long sigh. 'Bend at the waist. Come on, Mick, you're in this too. Let your whole body go forward and your hands hang down to the floor. Hold it there.'

'This is like PE, miss. Aren't we doing the play?'

Penny ignored Mick, and Bella frowned at him across the circle. Mick bent over. He stretched his fingers to the floor. Then he heard the back door of the hall open. He turned his head to see Masterman

78

come in and stand at the back. He folded his arms across his chest and leant back against the Honour Board that listed the ex-students who had died in the wars. Mick glanced at Penny.

'Bounce the top part of your body.' She appeared not to have noticed. 'Good. Good, well done, Tammy . . . And straighten up. Are you feeling relaxed?' She walked around them, touching them all lightly on the back or shoulders. They straightened up, grinning at each other and flexing the stretched muscles in their necks.

Except for Mick. He stood with his hands in his pockets and when she got near to him, said, 'I thought we were supposed to be singing. You said we had to sing.'

'I know. In a minute. You're all so uptight. Anyone would think this was an exam room. When you act, you have to be able to show your feelings. Let them out. You need relaxing.' Then she whispered, 'Don't worry about him.' She grinned at the larger group and then turned towards the back wall. 'Can we help you, Mr Masterman?' she called.

'No, Miss Lane.' He nodded politely. 'I just came in to see how you were getting on.'

'We're doing fine,' she said and turned back to the group. 'OK. This next exercise isn't hard, but some of you may find it tricky at first. Let's get in a circle.' She shepherded the group tightly.

Masterman walked across the back of the hall and out through a side door.

'I want one in the middle. How about you, Mick?'
He looked away.
She barely paused. 'You can have a turn later.

David? How about you?'

The boy who was to play Oliver stood in the centre.

'Right,' said Penny. 'I want you to fall – sideways, forwards, backwards. We'll catch you every time. Don't worry. We're here to support you.'

David looked at Mick. 'You'll just let me go,' he said.

'No, he won't,' said Penny. 'Will you?'

'I'll catch you, mate,' said Mick and he held his arms forward and buckled at the knee as if he was carrying a vast weight.

'I told you you could act,' said Penny.

'Here goes,' said David and toppled sideways against Mark, who caught him easily and pushed him back, upright. Down went David again, this time towards Penny and Tammy. They caught him, braced themselves for a moment and sent him back to the centre.

'This is great,' said David and flopped against Mick. Mick wasn't ready. He stumbled. For a second they looked as if they would both crash to the floor. Mark reached over and took some of the weight. That steadied them. Mick got his balance and almost threw David back to the centre of the ring.

'I had him,' he said looking up at the bigger boy, who shrugged and turned away.

'This last exercise is more individual,' said Penny. 'I want you to move around the room. By yourself. And I want you to concentrate very hard on one character. Concentrate so hard till you are that

80

character. So we don't spend too much time trying to work out who to be, I'm going to tell you. Girls, you can be your mother. Boys, your father.' She waved them out into the room. 'In a couple of minutes we'll come back to the centre and you can act the part for a minute or two. Do something that is typical of them.'

Mick watched as Mark and Margie moved away towards the windows. Tammy, her eyes closed, stood without moving, David was alongside him.

'You bloody near dropped me,' said David.

'Nah,' said Mick. 'Just mucking about.'

'Didn't feel like it.'

They stood together for a moment.

'I can't be my dad,' said Mick.

'Come on, you two,' said Penny. 'We don't have a lot of time.' She moved between them. 'Think of your dads. How do they walk? Where are their hands when they are talking? What do they say? Is there something funny they like doing?'

Mick shrugged. 'It's too hard, miss.'

'Rubbish. Close your eyes and concentrate. See him in every detail. In your mind, say Dad, Dad, Dad.'

Nine

Dad Dad Dad.

Be Dad. Walk like you . . . act like you . . . move my hands the way you do . . . Big hands spread wide over the steering wheel. So big they could crush a tennis ball. Thick sandy hairs. Sweat smell. Be you pulling hard on the brake, jumping down, squatting in the dirt. You slap the bonnet and it rings and clangs and you laugh.

Come on, Dad. Come home this weekend. We'll go to the weir like you said last time and you can fish. I'll swim and ride over the top on a sugar bag like you said you used to. I've never seen you do that. I'll be ready.

Mick's shoulders started to shake.

Be Dad. Eyes red from the dust and the drive. Tired. Always tired.

He moved further away from the group, stumbled against a chair and bent down to pick it up.

I can't be my dad.

'Where's he going?'

'Look, miss. Mick's clearing out.'

He reached the door. Penny's hands were on his shoulders.

'Why don't you go and get a drink of water? Don't worry about this exercise. We can start again later.'

Mick sat at the bottom of the steps, facing the patch of bush beside the science block. Penny came and sat beside him.

'It's nice and quiet when there's no kids around,' she said.

He didn't reply.

She leant forward, wrapping her arms around her knees. 'You don't want to do that exercise?'

'No.'

'Why not?'

He hesitated. 'Stupid.'

A pair of magpies flew down from the building and landed in the branches of the nearest gum tree. They threw their heads back and their warble, a rich sound deep in their throats, drifted across the playground.

'It may look stupid,' she spoke slowly, 'but we don't do anything without thinking about it first. There was a reason.'

'You said we were going to sing.' He watched the magpies.

'True. But you have to act as well, and to act, you have to relax and get into the character you're going to play.'

'But I'm not playing my dad.'

'No one's asking you to play your dad.'

'You just did.'

Penny sighed heavily and stood up. 'OK, OK. I meant in the play. This was only an exercise.'

She walked a few steps away and then turned back. 'They'll be finished now. Let's just forget about it and go in and see what's next.'

They went back into the hall. The year seven kids playing the workhouse children had arrived. Tammy, as the woman who looked after them, was on the stage, striding around with her imaginary bowl of gruel·and a huge ladle. Mick sat at the side, his arms folded, and watched as Bella and Penny took them through their routine.

I don't belong here. What am I doing?

Kids banged the tables and ate the slop that was served up to them. David, as Oliver, came forward and asked for more and then they danced through the songs that followed.

How did I end up doing this?

He leant back and half closed his eyes. The words were easy to follow. He suddenly realized that he knew them and he hadn't even tried to learn them at all.

In English Mick watched the clock getting closer to three fifteen. Ten more minutes. Then the decision – hang around and catch the last bus and hope that the others had gone earlier, or run for the first bus and hear them calling after him. There was a knock on the door and Masterman walked in. Mr Richards raised one eyebrow but stayed cool.

'Can I remind your boys, Mr Richards,' said Masterman, 'that anyone trying out for football teams is to come to a meeting straight after the bell.' He was looking at Tom and Danny in the back row. 'There are some very talented lads in this room.'

'Not only lads,' said Mr Richards. He slipped his hands into the pockets of his baggy cord trousers and glanced at Mick and then across at Tammy in the front row. 'And not just in football.'

Mick stood halfway down the aisle of the bus, balancing himself against the silver pole, his bag on his foot. Kids kept getting on. The sharp corner of a folder dug into his back.

'Watch it!' He turned around.

'Sorry. Oh, it's you, Mick.' Margie McGuire grinned at him. 'I've never seen you on this bus.'

'I usually go later,' he mumbled and pressed himself closer to the seats so she could get past.

'Don't know why I'm trying to move down there.' She planted her feet wide beside his as the bus started. 'There aren't any seats.'

'Got to be quick,' he said.

The bus stopped at the corner and then lurched forward again. She swayed but kept her balance, the folders in her arms pressing against the pole.

'God, we've got a lot of homework to do. And Penny wants us to learn all those lines by the end of the week.'

Mick shrugged. 'Not so bad for us. No exams I mean. My songs aren't too much. You've got loads more.'

'Keep me off the streets.' She grinned again. 'It's your first play, isn't it? It was great when we did one a few years ago. It was fantastic on opening night – everyone cheering at the end. We were so uptight beforehand. We were petrified we were going to make a mistake or forget a line. And we didn't make one. We had a great party afterwards. Mark says we can have one at his place after this show. You'll have to come. Mine's the next stop. See you at practice tomorrow.'

'See you.' He watched her get off and go down a side street beside the real estate office. The bus took off before he could see which way she turned next.

The next day Mick arrived first at lunchtime practice. He sat up the back of the hall, eating his apple, the words of his first song on his knee. After a few minutes, the rest of the cast drifted in. Margie arrived with Mark. She saw Mick and waved. He grinned at her. Tammy came in and sat down beside him.

'Know all your lines yet?' she said.

'No way.'

'I do. Mum sat up last night and took me right through them. You nervous?'

'Bit.'

'I could go through them with you sometime, if you like.'

'OK. Later.'

Penny and Bella arrived and they started work.

'I want you to imagine the set,' said Penny. 'The people building it have just started. We're going to have it on a couple of levels. Bits up high that give the feeling of old tenement houses, rooftops that you run across, stairways and so on. The feeling is busy, crowded – a huge nineteenth-century city of narrow streets, too many people – it's all a bit crazy. And I want you,' she looked at Mick, 'to be part of that craziness. You have to run a lot, tumble, do somersaults, throw yourself around the stage with a lot of energy.'

He rolled his eyes.

'Don't pull that face at me. I've seen you do this sort of thing. It'll be a piece of cake.'

'Fruitcake.'

'Nuts.' She waved to the gang members. 'You all have to be in on this business of fooling around. I want to see some life!'

Bella banged on the piano, Penny strode up and down across the room and the gang leapt and tumbled, leapfrogged and somersaulted on the stage. Mick led the singing, welcoming Oliver to the gang, teaching him how to pick pockets and then setting out on the day's work. He kept one eye on Penny's face as she called him in and directed him when to dart across the stage, when to pause and when to rouse his gang. Alan, as Fagin, rubbed his long hands in wicked glee, the last boy and girl disappeared into the wings and the whole cast collapsed on the floor in an exhausted heap.

'You knew them all the time!' said Tammy. She pushed Mick and he laughed and fell against Margie. She shoved him up into a sitting position.

'Not bad at all,' she said.

They drank from the jugs of iced water Penny had brought with her, and sat waiting.

'That was good,' she said. 'The bell's about to go so we haven't got much time. I wanted to tell you about something I thought of this morning. We're doing really well at all this. Bella and I are both pleased. We've got a suggestion though. We want you all to try to get further and further into the part that you're playing. Tonight I want you to write a piece of homework from the point of view of your character. It isn't actually compulsory. That means if you don't have time to do it, if you have too many other assignments, then forget about this. But – if you do have time, tear yourself away from the TV long enough. Sit down and *be* whoever you are supposed to be playing. Write some of your feelings as that character. Just what you've been doing today. Your day in the life of a London gang member. Try to imagine what that character would do and what they'd think about. It should be really helpful to feel the way your character would feel. OK? Any questions?'

'What do you mean?'

'Listen and I'll explain it once more.'

I'm the Dodger. The artful Dodger. I got up this morning and had breakfast. We had dried bread and a glass of gin. We left the house early to go and do some pickpocketting. We got this bloke out the front of the pub and he was half sozzled and I nicked a watch and wallet out of his pocket easy as falling off a log.

Mick sat back against the step and chewed on the end of his pencil. He had ripped a page from the ring-back exercise book he used for history. He played with the frayed edge. More fun than his real day. Seven periods of not speaking to Tom or Danny or Trev. Quoc sat with him in maths but that was just so he could show off his new calculator and then say no he couldn't borrow it. Recess it had rained and they'd stayed in close on the verandah. 'How's the play going?' Trisha had called. 'Signed up for Hollywood yet?' She'd only said it because Tom was near and somehow she thought she looked more beautiful when she laughed. Tom hadn't said a word to him. He'd spent the whole time talking to Danny and Trev. Mick had stood beside the verandah post, waiting for the bell and looking out for Tammy, the words of his songs going round in his head.

We – me and the new kid Oliver – went down to markets and stole some stuff for lunch. I had a pie and he got a couple of apples. Then we went all round the markets taking whatever we wanted. We got stuff to muck around with and money out of one bloke's box when he wasn't looking. Another bloke saw us and screamed out for someone to catch us but we got

away and laughed all the
way home. We had to
get the Money for Fagin
or there's nothing to
eat. He gets real cross
is we come home with
nothing.

Home. He closed his eyes and tried to see the tall
dark narrow tenements that Penny had showed in
the history book. But instead there was in his mind
a blur of a lawn with a lemon tree. Or maybe it was
orange. Tall, spiky grass. Then a dark place. A cool,
dark place. Cement floor. A boy crouching there,
holding something tightly to his chest.

Oliver hasn't got a mother either.

Why write that? None of the kids had any parents.
They just lived with Fagin. The way he lived with
Nan. No mother. No big deal. No need to go on
about it. He drew a line through it, then went over it
again, criss-crossing the space with thick black lines.

Dear Fran:

How about this. I'm writing in a free
period! Yes I feel guilty but no I am not
going to stop and do something else! It was
great to hear your voice the other night
when you rang. I thought it would be really
weird - my first birthday without all the
old crowd around - but Bella insisted we
go out to the local Vietnamese restaurant.
Food was great. We both pigged right out
and tried to forget we had to get up and
go to work the next day!

As to your thoughts about travel. Like I
said before - there seems to be so much
work I can't imagine that I'll feel ready to
go at the end of the year. It's nearly term
two already and I sometimes feel I've done
nothing!

The saga of the play continues! Was there
life before this? Loads of people helping
now. The Art department started on the set
this week and they've come up with great
designs. Gordon volunteered to be our stage
manager and he's helping with the direction
too. He's terrific to work with - so sane.
That's the way I'd like to be after fifteen
years in this job. (Ugh! What am I saying?)

Can you imagine what we'll be like by then?

But I did learn something the other day. I got the kids to act as if they were their own mother or father. Mick wouldn't do it. I should have guessed there'd be some weird stuff about his dad. Always wondered what I'd do when a kid said no! Made me feel helluva insensitive! Especially as he's been so good. He's rebuilt the model, he's there at every rehearsal - late sometimes - but he does make it. I even got accosted in the staffroom the other day by his maths teacher. This bloke reckons that since the play started, Mick has settled down and is working better than ever. I wait for the day when Masterman says the same thing!

Must go. I've got an eight o'clock start rehearsing the leading lady.

Penny

P.S. Sorry this letter is so caught up with work and the play. Truth is - nothing else going on in my life. Eligible males? Forget it! It seems all I think about is teaching and kids. Gordon says it's like this for everyone in their first year. I mean, I really like these kids, Fran, even the ones who don't like me or what I teach very much.

Ten

'Where's Masterman?' Danny yelled to Tom as he came towards the change room.

Mick, leaning against the wall, looked away.

'He's picking the squad this arvo. Davidson reckons he said that he's going to up the circuit training to five times around. He wants the fittest kids in the whole comp. Davidson says that he said we don't know what fitness is.'

Mick moved further away. Chris and Gerry van Dennis were talking near the door to the toilet block. They didn't like Masterman either. Five times round and Chris'd drop dead.

'Here he comes.' Gerry and Chris stood up.

Mick turned and watched as the PE teacher came down the steps from the top playground, two at a time. The sun glinted off the gold chain round his neck.

Mick picked up his bag, slung it over his shoulder and waited. At least he had clean shorts.

'Mr Masterman!' Margie McGuire called out from behind him.

The teacher had reached the boys. He stopped and waited as the girl came down the steps, her long black hair bouncing over her shoulders. When she got to the bottom he stood close to her while she talked so that no one could hear what she said.

Finally Masterman nodded and then the two of them came towards the group.

'Well, Jamieson. Smarten up. Tuck your shirt in. Can't have the big star of the show looking like something the cat dragged in.' He folded his arms. 'It appears the stars of our musical production are wanted for a photographic session with the local paper. You are to go with this young lady and it seems we are unlikely to have the pleasure of your company at all this lesson.' He turned his smile onto Margie. 'I don't know how we'll bear to be without him.'

She didn't smile back but looked him in the eye. 'I'm sure you'll survive. Come on, Mick. The others are waiting.'

They walked quickly up the steps together.

'God, he's sarcastic,' she said. 'How do you stand him?'

Mick shrugged. 'I don't.'

Penny and the others were waiting in the hall outside the principal's office. A man was there with a camera bag and a woman with a notebook. Mark was slicking his hair back in the glass of the painting that hung next to the trophy cabinet. Mick spat on his hand and smoothed back the bit of fringe that always got in his eyes. It fell forward again.

'Good,' Penny said to Margie. 'You found him.' She grinned at Mick. 'I hope you didn't mind missing PE.'

The group moved to the grassy spot under the windows of the staffroom. Mick knelt at the front with David and Tammy while Margie, Mark and the rest lined up behind. Mick felt Margie's legs brush against his back.

'OK,' said the photographer. 'Say cheese.'

'Sex,' said the group.

The camera clicked.

'Let's do something a bit informal,' said the photographer. 'Move in together.' He pushed them closer to each other and handed Penny a piece of paper. 'OK. All of you look at what she's holding. Pretend it's the words of a song.'

'Or a rave review in the national press,' said Penny.

Mick was squeezed between Margie and Brooke. His head came up to Margie's shoulder. Her hair blew across his face. It smelt warm and sweet and he wanted to reach out and touch it.

When the photographer had finished, the woman with the notebook called them all over to sit with her on the grass. First she wrote down their names and then she began to question them.

'I suppose you all had to try out for the show?'

'Yeah.'

'And you are all working hard learning songs and lines and stuff like that?'

'Yeah,' said Margie.

'What's the hardest part?'

'Fitting all that in with schoolwork. We hardly get out of anything. They're real slavedrivers.' Mark spoke and looked to the others. They all nodded.

'And the best part?'

'Having a good time.'

'Having fun.'

'Working with kids from different years. And with teachers in a way that's not like school usually.'

'Making new friends.' Margie looked at Mick and then at the others.

The woman turned to Mick. He hadn't said anything yet. 'What about you?'

He waited for a moment before he answered. 'Yeah. Making friends.'

The Easter holiday dragged.

At breakfast on Monday Nan looked up from her third cup of tea.

'Are you doing anything today?' she said.

Mick shrugged.

'I don't know what's going on with you,' said Nan. 'You've done nothing for the last few days but mooch around the house. Why don't you go over to Tom's? We never seem to see him at all these days.'

'He's got a girlfriend,' said Mick.

Nan raised her eyebrows. 'Well, what about the others?'

'No,' said Mick.

'Well, find something to do. I don't want you hanging around under my feet all day.'

Mick took the local phone book from the bookshelf and went into his bedroom. He turned to the 'M' pages. There was a whole column of McGuires. Which one? What was her father's name? Or her mother's? She got off the bus before him. That meant there were two possible suburbs. He took a sheet of paper from his school folder and started to write. Three names fitted. He found the local map and looked to see if any of the streets were near the real estate office where she got off the bus. One was in the street two blocks back from it. He wrote the number on the map.

The phone rang and he heard his grandmother come out of the kitchen to answer it.

'Mick,' she called, 'it's some girl wants to talk to you.' She raised her eyebrows and stood holding the receiver out to him.

Mick took it and waited till the kitchen door closed.

'Hello,' he said.

'Hello, it's Tammy here.'

'Oh.'

'I was wondering. Umm. Do you want to learn some lines? I mean, you know, go through the play. You could come over here . . . if you want to.'

'No. I can't. I'm busy today.'

She hung up quickly.

'I'm going out for a while, Nan,' he called.

He walked back the route of the school bus. Along the main road. There wasn't much traffic about. No buses. No trucks. It would take him twenty minutes. Then what? Knock on the door and ask for Margie? Wait outside and hope she'd come? What if she wasn't there? If she'd gone away for the break? He started to jog.

At the real estate office he stopped. He stood, his breath gradually slowing, and watched the two young girls on the upstairs balcony of the shop opposite. They looked about eleven. One was brushing the other one's hair. It was long and black and every now and then the wind caught bits of it and blew it out of reach. They were laughing and they looked up and saw Mick and pointed towards him and laughed some more.

He turned down the street that led to Margie's house.

It was brick, set back from the road with tall gum trees in the front yard. Mick walked past slowly. He dropped his map and bent down, facing the fence, to pick it up. The front curtains were open but he couldn't see anyone inside. In the driveway of the next house, a huge German shepherd lay, warm in the sun. Mick crossed the road to the corner shop and went in and bought himself a packet of chewing gum. He went back out to the footpath, leant against the shop window and watched the house. After ten minutes he went into the shop again and bought more gum, this time with football cards. He sat in the gutter and sorted the cards, one eye on the house.

A car pulled up. Margie was in the front seat. Mick jumped up and ducked back into the shop. He stood near the window, watching and trying to look as if he was reading the sporting magazine.

'Can I help you?'

'Just looking.'

He tried to peer through the cigarette advertisements.

He didn't recognize the driver.

Margie got out and stood on the footpath. She was wearing tennis clothes and carrying a racket. The driver came around the front of the car and put his arm across her shoulders. He said something and she laughed and ducked away from him. He grabbed her hand and their fingers stayed locked together as they went up into the house.

Mick dropped his cards. He heard the front door of the house slam. He knelt on the floor, picking up the pieces of cardboard. He didn't want them. He hadn't collected any for three years. Even then he hadn't really cared. He dumped them in the bin as he walked away.

Eleven

'OK. Everyone. You've had a few days off and now it's time for some hard work. We're going to do the song that opens the second act. Where Dodger and Nancy entertain all the gang at Fagin's by showing them how the upper classes treat each other. Mick, Margie. This is your big number together.'

Penny beckoned them up onto the stage with her.

Mick wouldn't look at Margie but moved to stand close to Penny.

'You others are on stage at the same time and you join in on the chorus but I want these two to get it right first.' She dropped her voice to speak just to them. 'You've been practising with Bella. Are you ready now?'

They both nodded.

'Have you thought about how we should do it?'

Mick shrugged. 'Not really. I s'pose I should just go back across the stage a few times. Sort of acting to the other kids – like they're the audience.'

'OK.' Penny nodded. 'It's a send-up. Right? You can't stand the upper classes. You despise them. You are laughing at the way a gentleman treats his lady. Overact. Go down on your knees. Kiss the hem of her dress if you like.'

Mick screwed his face up.

'Not her skirt. Her long dress on the night. Lots of

bowing and la-di-da-ing.' Penny turned to Margie.
'And what about you?'

'I thought I should prance around a bit with my
nose in the air. Plum in my mouth. You know.
Maybe we could walk up and down with our arms
linked and he could have a walking stick and a
pretend top hat and be taking it off and putting it
back on. Stuff like that.'

'Sounds good to start with.' Penny waved to Bella
and the music began.

'Come on, Dodge. Shall we show 'em how it's done,'
sang Margie. *'It's all bowing and hats off.'*

*'And don't let your petticoat dangle in the mud, my
darling . . . '* sang Mick.

'Stop. Stop it right there.' Penny stood in front of
Mick. 'What's up with you? A few days' break and
you're all wooden. Stiff. Come on. Look at her.
She's not going to bite your head off. You've got to
act like you're in love with her.'

Mick looked away.

In love with her. Penny's voice echoed off the high
stage ceiling.

He studied his bare feet; the Bandaid across his left
ankle, the frayed white edges of his jeans.

'Come on, you've done it before.'

Kids in the front row where whispering, rustling
papers.

Bella played the tune softly, one finger.

'Be like you were last time.'

He turned round slowly and looked up at Margie.
She stood with one arm stretched out to him while
the other gathered up layers of petticoat and skirt.

'OK.' He took off an imaginary top hat and bent over with an exaggerated flourish. He bowed to the audience of Fagin's gang. He gave Margie his arm and led her across the stage. His strong voice filled the hall, and the workhouse kids up the back stopped their whispering and listened, staring. He finished the song on his knees, arms outstretched, gazing up at the girl in front of him.

'Bravo! Well done.' Penny was clapping loudly. So was Tammy, who was sitting in the front row. Bella grinned from behind the piano.

'That was great,' whispered Margie.

'It's going well,' Penny said to him as they walked out of the hall together.

Mick nodded.

'We've only got a few weeks to go. I think we're going to make it.'

'No worries.'

'Touch wood!' She flicked the door frame and then touched him on the back of the head. 'Remember – tomorrow, I want you word perfect and no scripts.'

He left her at the bottom of the steps and ran to the bus stop. Margie was waiting by herself, a short distance away from the others. Mick hesitated. She saw him and called him over.

'You catching the bus?' she said.

'Yeah.' He dropped his bag and leant against the warm brick wall and closed his eyes.

'You were great today.'

'Thanks.' He kept his eyes shut. He didn't know what to say.

'Is your nan going to come and see the play?'

'I s'pose so. We haven't talked about it. She will, but . . .'

She'd said she would back at the start. She'd written to Dad to let him know but they hadn't heard from him since.

'My mum and dad are going to. And my sisters. They don't live at home any more but they're both coming. I think Mum's going to buy tickets for the whole street. She's like that. When they took our photo for the paper, she went out and bought about a dozen. Every living relative got one!'

Mick opened his eyes.

Margie was grinning as she talked. 'She'll probably sit in the front row and clap like mad every time I even look like opening my mouth. She's so embarrassing!'

'Unreal.'

They laughed.

'My nan wouldn't do that,' said Mick. 'Thank God.'

He left the bus and headed up and over the footbridge.

She's so embarrassing. But when Margie spoke about her mum she sounded pleased.

Was my mother like Margie's? Photos don't tell.

He is five years old. He is leading the Easter hat parade. His green cardboard hat with its stuck-on eggs is so tall and so heavy that it keeps falling forward and he has to hold it with one hand. Dad is away but she is out there, watching. On his first day at school she took him on the bus and then sat and waited until the woman in charge was ready to interview her. Mick sat with two other boys and a girl on a hard wooden bench outside the office. He can smell the corridor. He can even see the colour of the paint on the wall.

He kicked the railing. Below him, a silver Volvo swerved around an open utility. It sped ahead and was almost out of sight by the time he reached the top. Funny that he had sat here, tossing coins, trying to decide if he should go in the play. He ran his hand along the rail as he walked. Word perfect, Penny said. You were great, Margie said. He knew his part nearly backwards. Hadn't used a script for the last two practices. Only missed one cue this afternoon and that wasn't really his fault. He went down two steps at a time and then cleared the last four in a single go.

The Mack was parked outside the house. It towered over the red Cortina parked in front of Lees' place. It almost reached the top of the tree outside Calvaros's place. Sun glinted off the chrome at the top and off the windscreen.

Mick ran the last two blocks. He leapt up the steps at the back and slid his bag across the kitchen floor.

'Where is he?'

Nan came down the hall.

'When did he get here?'

'Ssh.' She put her finger to her lips. 'He's asleep. He's been driving all night.' She pushed him into the kitchen and closed the door. 'He was just wrecked when he got here.'

'Where did he come from last night? How long is he staying?' Mick couldn't sit down.

'He came in after lunch,' said Nan. 'He's been asleep nearly ever since.'

'Why didn't he say he was coming? I'd've stayed home.'

Mick went out the front and walked around the huge truck. He climbed up on the step and tried the door. It was locked. He peered in. His father's sunglasses lay on the passenger seat on top of a newspaper and a screwed-up chocolate wrapper. He went round to the driver's side. That door was open. He climbed in and sat still for a moment on the seat that was hot from the sun. He ran his eyes across all the dials and switches, the box of tapes neatly stacked in the glovebox, the papers and pens in the clear folder on the dashboard. He put on the glasses and leant forward so that his elbows rested on the lower rim of the wheel. His feet hung above the foot pedals.

Brmm brmm. Press the foot down. Fifty ks to go. Got to get to Sydney on time. Got to see my son's show. He's a star, you know. Big production. Brmm. Brmm. Got me a front-row seat. Opening night tonight. Brmm.

Mick could see across the tops of the gardens for two blocks. Below him, Mrs Calvaros came out to the gate and checked the mailbox. She looked up and down the street but didn't notice him. Mr Lee's grey Datsun, the top scratched and stained, pulled up across the footpath in front of his house. He got out to open the gate and his big white dog leapt up at him from the other side of the fence.

Mick grabbed the wheel and tried to turn it. He closed his eyes.

The curtain falls. Loud cheers. Clapping. People everywhere. C'mon, Dad. Come and meet Penny. Penny, this is my dad, Max. He's come all the way from Queensland to see the play . . . and this is Margie . . . Tammy . . . Mark . . .

Mick went into the laundry to wash his hands for tea. He stepped over his father's clothes, a huge pile of singlets, socks and underpants, tee shirts, shorts and grease-covered overalls. He breathed in deeply. He grinned as he shook his wet hands over them. In the kitchen, the smells of his father mixed with the smell of chops and onions and boiling vegetables.

'I don't know when he'll wake up.' Nan shrugged as she smoothed the tablecloth and put a plate of food in front of Mick. 'He could sleep right through.'

'Have you talked to him about the play?'

'Sort of. I told him you were in one. I didn't say anything about him coming.'

'Did he?'

'Mick, I told you. He was wrecked when he came in. We didn't talk much at all.' She started to eat. 'Ask him later. I'm sure he'll come if he can.'

After tea, Mick couldn't keep still. He hung around Nan while she finished the ironing and again when she made a cup of tea and sat down to do the crossword. He crept out to the side yard and peered through the spare room window. When his eyes got used to the light, he saw his father as a large dark shadow in a sleeping bag on top of the bed. Mick went back into the kitchen.

'Haven't you got any homework?' Nan said.

'No.'

'Well you must have lines to learn for the play.'

'I know them all. Do you reckon he'll come?'

She didn't answer.

He stood for a moment outside the door to the spare bedroom.

Wake up, Dad. Come and have tea and I'll sit across from you and I'll tell you about the play and who's in it and . . .

He went into his own room to the bookcase. The football trophy was sitting on top of a couple of magazines. He cleared them away and placed the trophy in the centre of the top shelf. He took a *Wheels* magazine and flopped on the bed. Trucks, four-wheel drives, utes. He flicked through the pages of glossy photographs and bold headlines. *Lean Machines. Keep on Truckin'. King of the Road.*

He went back out to the lounge room.

'Can't we wake him up, Nan?'

She shook her head.

'I wouldn't do that. You don't want to get him angry. You're just going to have to wait till morning.'

Dear Fran:

Boy, did I get a shock when I opened your
letter this morning. What do you mean
you're going to quit? Is it really as bad as
all that? I suppose I'm just confused
because in the beginning you seemed so
happy and sure that you were in the right
job. I know you said you didn't get on with
a few people up there and I know you've
been a bit lonely ... but if you quit now,
what will you do? Have you got any money?
Are you going to travel? On what? Go back
to study? Do you want to come down here
for a bit - just till you work yourself out?

I guess one reason that I feel so
differently to you is that I'm having such
a ball with this play. I really am. At first I
thought it was great for the kids - and
that is true - but it's also great for us. I
love watching them get on top of everything
They've all come along tremendously. It's
word perfect time tomorrow and I'm quite
confident they'll be fine. Mick especially.
You know I have such a soft spot for that
kid. He has matured out of sight. At the
year meeting earlier this week I had almost
everyone complimenting me on his improved
attitude. I felt a bit like a mother at a
parent teacher night! I don't want to take

credit but it is good. He'll probably lapse after the show, but still ...

Bella and I are so far into this play routine that we think we'll go one better next year. She reckons we could prepare the kids for the big rock eisteddfod. Move over traditional school plays! If this one freaked out the staff, imagine what a rock performance will do! Needless to say we haven't told anyone yet. Gordon will be in it. The kids'll love it.

Enough ramblings. We're in the middle of assessments so I've got a pile of marking to do. Sometimes I wish I was a full time drama teacher - at least that would mean an easier work load. And the trouble is, I've been raving on to the kids in the play about doing all their work as well - so I can't let mine get behind.

Let me know if you change your mind about leaving. Maybe you could head for London and get a job and get set up ready for when I come after next year?

Love,
Penny

Twelve

'Where is he?' Mick raced into the kitchen.

'It's OK. He's gone for a run to get the paper. He won't be long.'

Back in his room, Mick pulled on his jeans. Forget school, stay with Dad. Footsteps on the gravel strip outside made him jump. He strained to hear the squeak of the gate or steps on the verandah. When they came, he hesitated. He fumbled the last button on his shirt and ran his fingers through his hair.

His father stood in the doorway, leaning on the frame, newspaper tucked under his arm.

'G'day, son.'

'G'day, Dad.'

'Coming to breakfast?'

Mick nodded and they walked down the hallway together. The man resting his hand lightly on the boy's shoulder.

Mick poured milk on his cereal and watched while his father ate scrambled eggs on toast and drank two cups of coffee. He had curly blond hair that fell into his eyes when he dropped his head. There was a gold signet ring on the little finger of his right hand. Mick couldn't remember it from before, but the freckles that shone through the pale hairs on his knuckles were the same. So was the scar above his left eye.

'C'mon, son. Eat up.'

Mick turned to his own breakfast but kept glancing up as his father flicked through the paper.

'Did you have a good trip, Dad?'

'Not bad.'

'Did you come on the highway or down the coast road?'

'The highway. It's getting better.'

'How long are you down for?'

'Depends.'

They sat in silence for a moment.

'Dad.'

'Mm.'

'D'you want to go fishing like you said you would last time? Down at the weir? I don't have to go to school.'

His father shook his head. 'No. Not today. I've got some stuff to do.'

'Well, what about you drive me to school? Take me in the truck.' Arrive in the big rig. Blast the horn. See Tom. See all you lot. Jump down from the cabin and wave back at Dad.

'No way, Mick. It needs a bit of work on it and then I have to see someone about some business.'

Mick slumped back in his chair.

'Well, if you have to go somewhere, can't I come with you?'

His father shook his head. He put his newspaper down and looked at Mick.

'Sorry, mate. Nan tells me school's going all right.'

Mick shrugged.

'You keeping out of trouble OK?'

'Yeah.'

'She tells me you're in a play.'

'Yeah. I've got to sing on my own.'

'Sooner you than me, mate.'

'Can you come, Dad?' Mick leant forward. Tell him he had to come. Tell him everyone's mum and dad were coming. Margie's mum was coming every night. 'It's going to be great.'

'Settle down, mate.' His father pushed his chair back. 'I don't know.'

'But not even for one night? It'll be at a weekend.'

'I've got to work, son.'

'Can't you . . . ?'

'I'm a working man, Mick. I can't just stick around whenever I feel like it. When your play is on, I could be anywhere.'

'Can't you get a run back here?'

'It's not always that easy. I'll probably be back up north.'

'But I haven't even told you when it is.'

'You don't have to. If this bloke I'm seeing today can get me a load, I could even be heading out again tonight, late.'

Mick clenched his spoon. 'Just this once. Can't you . . . ?'

'I would if I could. Your nan'll come. She'll tell me how you went.'

'I don't want just Nan to come. You could come if you wanted to. When you're grown up you can do anything.' Mick banged his spoon against his plate.

His father slapped his hand on the table. 'Jesus! When are you going to grow up? I'm working long

112

and hard to keep you down here and at school. OK, I like driving. It's what I want to do. But don't kid yourself. There's not much money in it. I don't get too much say. You take the job when you can and you go for it. If I say I can't be here it's because I can't be here.' He folded his paper and stood up. 'I'm sorry about it, Mick, but I can't do anything to change it.' He took his wallet and keys from the sideboard. 'I'll see you later.'

Mick went into his bedroom. 'I hate him,' he yelled. 'I hate him. I hate him. I hate him.' He picked up the trophy from the bookcase and hurled it through the open window. It crashed against the trunk of the lemon tree.

'You'd better get ready for school,' Nan called. She had come out of the kitchen and was standing in the doorway. 'Don't worry about him, love. I'll have a talk to him. Haven't you got a big practice of the play today?'

Mick bashed his fist down hard on the windowsill.

'Stuff him and stuff the play. I'm not doing it.'

'Michael!' She grabbed him by the shoulders and pushed him against the wardrobe. 'Don't let me hear you speak like that. He isn't round much, but he is your father and he's a good hard-working man. Don't you make him your reason for doing it or not doing it. This is your show. You said you'd do it.'

I'm not doing it.

Mick shoved his school clothes into the back of the wardrobe, put all the money he could find into his pockets and went out the front door. And I'm not going to school. The truck stretched the width of the house. He walked slowly round it. He kicked the tyres. Bend down. Let the air out. All twenty-four of them. Then run like hell and never come back. Would he care? Would he notice? He slapped his hand on the warm metal of the driver's door and threw a final kick at the nearside wheel.

Nick's brother Stavros was washing his car.

'Hi,' he said. 'Gee, you're going to be late.'

'Going into town,' said Mick.

He hadn't really thought about it till then. Going into town. Not such a bad idea. No Dad. No one to ask about homework. No Tom and his mates to hide from. No play practice. No Margie with her face all smiles like she really cared when . . . He started to jog. Funny how he quite liked running when Masterman wasn't around. He concentrated on his breathing. It was past nine o'clock already. English first lesson. Richards would notice he wasn't there. He'd tell Penny in the staffroom at recess.

I'm not doing it.

He ran on in the cool morning. Onto the footbridge. Up the steps. He stopped at the top. He couldn't think and run at the same time. He gripped the rails. I mean it. If he's too busy to come. He looked across to the city. The centre was lost in a blue-brown autumn haze.

A truck beneath him roared, smoke pouring from its stack.

He ran down the other side of the footbridge, climbed the rail onto the freeway and started to walk towards the city. No one stopped to pick him up. He waved his thumb and turned to look over his shoulder. A shimmering blue Mercedes with only one person in it. The driver looked away. A white van with Queensland plates. Probably heading for Brisbane. Dad wouldn't leave till tonight. Race him all the way. Get there first. Sneak into the old house. Wait there like the old days, with Mum.

He is seven years old. He sits in the lowest branch of the jacaranda tree. He's coming, Mum, he calls as the shiny silver truck turns the corner at the bottom of the hill.

A couple of cars were racing along in the far lane. Trucks revved their engines way behind him. He'd never hitchhiked on the freeway before. Tom had once but the police had picked him up and warned him that if they got him again, they'd book him. At least that's what Tom said. Mick kicked a stone and it rattled into the drain. Probably lying. Maybe everything Tom ever said was bullshit. All that stuff about fights and girls. Except Trisha. That was plain for everyone to see. They all lied. Dad too. Your mother's just going into hospital for a while, he'd said. The doctors'll make her better. Without your mother I just can't manage. I'm on the road the whole time. I can't do any other job. Nan'll look after you. I'll come whenever I can. But more and more often his trips went further north. To Cairns. To Townsville and then west to Mt Isa. More money he said. Less competition. What if he didn't want to come?

After three quarters of an hour, his feet were sore

and still no one had stopped. He had gone under two more footbridges and the last exit to the mountains. The next one was the truckstop. Lunch. A meat pie, some lollies and a lift into town. He was limping slightly as he turned into the exit ramp.

The pie was lukewarm but he emptied the whole container of tomato sauce onto it and sat by the window to watch the trucks come in. There were four already, parked at the side, their drivers gathered around the video machines at the far end of the room. They were laughing and drinking and they cheered when the one at the controls made a score.

That time. Coming down to Nan's. Mick sat on the counter and ate hot chips and Dad played with the guy who drove the Shell tanker. The other guy won and Dad said he was off his game and anyway they had to keep moving.

Go up to them. Ask if they are going into the city. But Mick stayed in his seat, licking the tomato sauce from his fingers and sucking the last of his juice through the straw.

'Anything else?' The waitress stood at the end of his table, her eyebrows raised.

Mick shook his head and turned back to the window.

The woman sat down across the table from him.

'D'you reckon one of those blokes would give me a ride into town?' he said.

She shrugged. 'Might. You could ask.'

'D'you know them?'

She nodded.

'Would you ask them for me?'

'Depends.' She paused. 'Depends on what you're going into town for.'

'Christmas shopping.'

'Give over.' She rolled her eyes to the ceiling and then looked directly at him. 'Don't get smart with me, sunshine. There's too many like you running around in there with nowhere to go and nothing to eat.' She dropped her voice. 'You in trouble? Your old man been belting you around?'

Mick shook his head.

'No.'

'Well, why don't you just go on home to your mum then?'

''Cause I haven't got one.'

'Jesus! Me and my big mouth.' Her eyebrows furrowed and she reached forward to take his hand. He pulled it away. She went to the kitchen and came back with a pot of tea, two cups and a plate of cakes. 'It's on the house,' she whispered as she went back to serve another customer.

'So, will you tell me where you're going and why?' she asked when she finally came back and sat down. She pushed a thick piece of chocolate cake towards him. The icing was almost black and there were slivers of orange pressed down into it. She looked old enough to have kids in high school.

'What's wrong?'

'Nothing.'

'Nothing! You've got a face as long as a wet week. I'm not gunna dob you in. You can tell me.'

He chewed the cake slowly. Tell her. But what? Dad won't come to the play so I'm chucking it in. Sounds pretty slack. Clearing out. But that's not true. I'm just missing a day. And I'm not doing the play.

'Have you got any kids?'

'Yeah. A couple.'

'If one of them was in a play, would you go and see it?'

'Yeah.' She looked at him cautiously.

'What if you had to work?'

'I'd try and change my shift. Get someone to work for me.'

'And if no one would?'

She didn't answer for a moment. She picked up some of the cake crumbs and rolled them between her thumb and forefinger. 'I'd probably take a sickie. Lose pay. If it meant that much to him.'

If it meant that much to him.

Did it mean that much? What did Margie say? . . . Fantastic on opening night . . . better than winning trophies . . . that great gut feeling. And Penny . . . I put myself on the line for you . . . Why can't Dad put himself on the line . . . why can't he see how much . . . ?

Mick looked at his watch and then outside. It was starting to rain. They'd be in the music room. Penny looking at her watch. Have you seen Mick? she'd say to no one in particular. And then she'd say it directly to each of the others and they'd all say no. Margie might screw her face up. Would she care, though, or just be fed up because they couldn't do their song? Tammy'd say that he wasn't in any classes. She'd

rung him to go and practise with her. Why? Penny'd
get cranky or worried that he was sick and she'd talk
to Bella about it and then they'd go on to a section
that he wasn't in. But today was the day to be word
perfect. I think we're going to make it. No worries.

Mick's head slumped forward. He clenched his
fists. I am not going to do it.

This is your show. You said you'd do it.

He knew that he would.

When he looked up, the waitress was still sitting
facing him. The rain was still falling. The men had
stopped playing the machines and were outside,
turning the big trucks round, getting ready to go.
One was already on the road.

Mick jumped up.

'Where are you going?' she said.

'I've got to go. I've got to get to practice.' And he
ran out into the rain, calling and waving to the driver
of the last rig who was just climbing into the cabin.

Thirteen

'You are late.' Penny stood at the bottom of the stairs that led to the music room.

'I'm sorry, I . . .' He was puffing. He'd run all the way from the top gate and he had a stitch in his left side. He bent over to catch his breath.

'You needn't bother to go in. Bella's rearranged the rehearsal. She's working with the others. She doesn't need you.'

'It was . . .'

'I'm not interested in excuses, Michael. You were supposed to be at rehearsal.' She stopped and blew her nose. Her face was red and her voice was louder than usual.

'I tried to get back.'

'You have been wagging school all day. No, you just listen to me. I put myself on the line for you. I swore to everyone in this place that you were right for this role and that you would perform. I stood up for you when they were all out baying for your blood. And you repay me like this. You let me down. You let down the rest of the cast.'

Ratbag. Bludger. Boy like this just lets you down.

'You knew this was an important rehearsal. When I found out you weren't at school today I assumed you were sick and I rang to see if you could come in just for the session this afternoon. Your grandmother says you left the house early to come to school. I said I must have made a mistake and that you would be around somewhere. But you weren't.' She was yelling at him now. 'I am fed up, Mick. Fed up.'

He yelled back at her. 'Why don't you listen to me?'

'I am sick of listening to you. I listen to you too much.' She waved her hand at him. 'Take yourself home now and bring your excuses to me in the morning. And they'd better be good.'

She started to walk away.

He screamed after her. 'You're just like bloody Masterman. You act all friendly but you're all . . . you're all just like bloody Masterman.'

Mick sat in the gutter out the front of the school. The last bus had gone some time ago and the only cars in the car park belonged to the people at rehearsal.

He stood up, thrust his hands deep into his pockets and kicked at the stones in his way. The rain was starting again, small fine drops like mist that he ignored as they settled lightly on his face.

He walked down to the old main road and hesitated. Sydney was twenty-five kilometres away. He wrapped his fingers around a twenty-cent piece. Heads, hitch a ride into the centre of the city. Tails, go home. The morning seemed a hundred years ago. Dad might have changed his mind. Maybe he couldn't get a load. Mick turned his back on the city and quickened his step. Cars raced past spraying water from the puddles on the side of the road. The rain, heavy now, blew in sheets against his skin. He hunched his shoulders and felt the water running down the inside of his collar. He pressed his body against a shopfront.

A car cruised slowly behind him, drew alongside and stopped. Penny opened the passenger door.

'I want to talk to you,' she said.

He started to walk on. She drove alongside and sounded the horn.

'Get in and I'll drive you home.'

He got in the front and sat as far away from her as possible. She didn't drive off but reached into her jacket pocket and took out a couple of Minties.

'Here, have one of these,' she said. 'I've been thinking. I should have given you time to explain. It was wrong of me not to listen.'

He sucked on the Mintie and screwed up the lolly paper and dropped it on the floor. He shuffled his feet and kicked the paper under the seat. Then he looked up at her. 'I shouldn't have said that about Masterman. It's not true. You're not like that.'

'Well. Let's not talk about him. Do you want to say something about what happened today?'

He stared at the rain washing down over the windscreen. He felt cold and hungry and tired.

'Dad came down last night.'

'That's good.'

'He says he can't come to the play.'

'I see . . . I'm sorry.'

'I just got so wild at him. I took off.'

'Where did you go?'

'I was gunna go into the city.'

'Did you?'

'No.'

122

The waitress brought him cake. I'd take a sickie. Lose pay. If it meant that much to him.

'I'm still wild at him. He could come if he really wanted to. If he knew how much . . . I told Nan I wasn't going to go in it any more.'

Penny's hands tightened on the wheel. She sniffed and then fiddled with a knob on the dashboard and the only sound in the car was the swishing of the windscreen wipers.

She turned to him. 'And – are you?'

'Yeah, I s'pose so. No point wasting all that practice.'

Mick lay on his bed and listened. He heard the television down the hall, a car two streets away, the creak of boards as Nan crossed from the lounge room to the kitchen. The light from the street lamp lit up the bare top of the bookcase. He half thought of getting out of bed and going to find the trophy from under the lemon tree but he couldn't be bothered.

Dad hadn't come home for tea.

'He'll be in late,' said Nan. 'And then he might be going again before breakfast.'

'Has he changed his mind about the play?'

'He didn't say. I did talk to him, though. I let him know how much work you'd put into it. And I gave him the photo that was in the paper.' She stopped clearing the table. 'He put it in his wallet. He is proud of you, Mick. He mightn't show it too well. You mustn't let him stop you. You're star of your own show now – and I'm not just talking about the play.'

A car pulled up outside. A door slammed. Low voices. The gate squeaked. Mick held his breath as the front door opened and closed. He felt his father come into the room.

'You still awake?'

'Yes,' Mick whispered.

His father didn't turn the light on but tiptoed across to the bed and sat down.

'I've been thinking, mate, about this morning.'

Mick lay perfectly still.

Take a sickie. Lose a day's pay.

'I'm really sorry. I mean, I don't get to see you too often, what with work and all. It's stupid to spend that time fighting and arguing.'

Say you'll come. Go up to Brisbane in the morning but then come back for the play. I didn't mean it when I said I wouldn't do it.

'I've been thinking all day about missing your play and about this whole business – the way you live down here with Nan and I'm up there in Brisbane. I can't move back down here, mate. Everything – all my contacts are there. I'd take a huge loss if I came back here. And I just can't get enough work staying in town all the time to have you living with me. I just hope you can understand. It was hard enough when your mother was alive – me being away so much. You were so close to her. It was great when I'd get back from a run.'

He sat there in the half light, staring at his hands in his lap. The fingers were interlocked, but he was rubbing the palms together all the time as he spoke.

Say it, Dad. Say it.

'But since she . . . well . . . ' He turned and faced Mick. 'Dammit, Mick, you never showed anything when it happened. If you'd cried or said something I might've known what to do with you.'

No, Dad. Don't.

'You hid out the whole time I was at the funeral. You wouldn't talk to me or to Mrs Jackson.'

I didn't. I don't remember.

'You never mentioned it afterwards. The whole bloody time. You wouldn't talk to me, wouldn't show a thing.'

But I don't know what happened. You didn't tell me. You said she was getting better. She said she was getting better. You all lied. And now I try to remember and there's nothing there.

Cold, hard cement floor.

'I didn't know what you were thinking or how to handle you or even if you were OK. I had to bring you down here.'

He stood up and walked over to the window and sat down on the sill.

'Hey, what have you done with that old footie trophy I gave you? I thought it was on the bookcase.'

'It's around somewhere.'

'Are you playing this year? I'll give you a few tips. We'll have a kick around in the park . . . '

The play, Dad. What about the play?

'. . . Next time I come down, I'll make sure I can stay a few days. Or we could do it in the holidays. You come up to me. I'll send the fare. I'll have some time off and we'll go into town and watch a match. I'm not making a good job of telling you all this. But I do worry about you and I think about you.'

Mick shifted slightly under the blankets.

'There's no way out of it till you're older. I'm not having you running wild up there. I'll keep coming down when I can.'

Mick raised himself on one elbow.

'So you won't make it down for the play, will you?'

'Like I said this morning, it's impossible.'

Dear Fran:

Are you sitting down? I'm quitting. Leaving.
Coming with you - wherever that is. I take
back everything I said last letter. I've had
enough and that's what I've decided to do.
Like you, I'm going to teach till early
September and then that's it.

It's so sudden that I'm still trying to
justify it to myself. Part of it is work. I'm
just tired all the time. I never seem to stop
or get a minute for myself. I was late
getting one group of assessments in and I
copped it from the Assistant Principal. How
dare he - just because he's ex-technical
subjects where there's no real marking to
do. I had over a hundred essays last
weekend. And I had a parent in here the
other day telling me how easy we get it.

The rehearsal yesterday that was supposed
to be everyone word perfect was a mess.
Gordon put his glasses on a seat and I sat
on them and broke them, the kid playing
Oliver has laryngitis and will make the
performance only if he doesn't sing a note
till the night, and to cap it all, Mick didn't
show. It was the moment I've been dreading
all year - the moment to admit that maybe I
was wrong and they - all those who said he

wouldn't do it - were right. I could just see the patronising sneer on Masterman's face. Creep. And the thought of drafting another kid into the role...

He showed up in the end. I wasn't very sympathetic. How do I get myself into these things? Why can't I just come along, teach and then go home?

Anyway, I've got a lousy cold and to cap it all, I got to school this morning and who should I run into in the car park but Masterman. He must have known about yesterday because he gave me this patronising smile and said, `I believe you're having some problems with young Jamieson. Perhaps now you know what I meant.' `Problems, Mr Masterman?' I said, and smiled sweetly. You'd've been proud of me Fran. It was the coldest, bitchiest tone of voice. `I don't know what you're talking about.'

And then I thought - you're not getting away with this, and I went up, I stood in front of him, and I told him exactly what I thought of him. That he was insensitive, he didn't care about kids and that I found his attitude appalling.

I thought he was going to hit me. He was absolutely stunned. Speechless. I just walked off. But I can't stand it, Fran. When the play is over I'm going to retreat to my corner and look after <u>me</u> for a change and when third term's finished, I'm off.

I told Gordon this afternoon. He says I'll get over it, that I'm just depressed and that in a day or two I might feel differently. I don't think so.

After the fiasco yesterday I've got the leading lady to keep an eye on Mick on the night. She says she'll watch him from the minute we arrive till curtain up. Fingers crossed nothing goes wrong.

Sorry if this is a bit depressing. I'm sure I'll feel better when the cold has gone. But I'm not going to change my mind. Write and tell me your plans and let's see if we can organize something together.

Love,
Penny

Fourteen

Mick was early. He leant against the telegraph pole outside the darkened hall and looked at the café across the road. He saw warm orange lights, smelt chicken and chips and heard laughter and the ringing sound of the pinball machine. He picked up his bag and started across the road.

'Mick. Hang on, mate.'

Alan called to him from the corner. Mick turned and saw him, walking with Mark and Margie.

'You looked like you were clearing out,' said Margie.

Mick shook his head. 'Just thought I'd go and feed the animals churning round in my guts.'

'Butterflies?'

'Kangaroos playing leapfrog, more likely.'

'And you want to feed them?' said Alan. 'It'll make you want to chuck up on stage. Imagine that.'

He leapt up onto the low brick wall and stretched his arms out.

'*Consider yourself, our mate* . . . chunder chunder *Consider yourself one of the family* . . . spew spew.'

He clutched his stomach, twisted his face and poked his tongue out. 'Yuk.'

A car swung round the corner and stopped under the streetlight.

'Are you all right?' Penny called from the driver's

side. 'What's up?'

Alan stepped down and bowed.

'Just part of the performance, ma'am.'

'Save it for the audience.' She grinned and shook her head. 'Are you all ready? God, I'll be glad when this is over.'

In the dressing room, Mick sat with Margie in front of an old wardrobe mirror. It was laid on its side on top of a table.

'We've got fifteen minutes,' she said, 'and then it's Alan's and Mark's turn.'

She looked through the mass of jars of different colour make-up, trays of eyeshadows, thick black and brown pencils and cans of hairspray. She patted heavy make-up over her face. He rubbed a handful of cold cream through his hair and pulled the spikes forward. He glanced at her as she spread green shadow on her eyelids, painted thick black lines around her eyes and put a spot on her cheek.

'You need a bit too,' she grinned.

He looked away. 'Penny said all I had to have was a bit of dirt.'

'Let me.' Margie swung her chair around till her face was close to his. She dabbed liquid make-up onto his forehead and cheeks. Then she smoothed it over his skin, her long fingers cool and slow.

'Hey,' she said. 'You've got a beaut scar there, near your eyebrow. I've never noticed that before. Your hair's always in the way.'

'Fell out of a tree,' said Mick. 'When I was about seven. Used to sit in this tree all day waiting for Dad to come home from a run.'

131

'Can he make it tonight?'

'No.' He was quiet for a moment but then he said, 'He's somewhere out near the Northern Territory. Sent me a postcard though. First one I've had in ages. Had crocodiles on it. Must think I'm still a little kid.' Mick laughed and then looked at her as she brushed her hair with long strokes.

'I didn't know you played tennis.'

'Yeah, every weekend. How do you know?'

'Oh, I saw you one day. At Easter.'

'We played competition three days in a row.' She grinned at him in the mirror. 'You are looking at one half of the local mixed doubles, A-grade champion.'

'Who's the other half?'

She dabbed rouge on her cheeks and paused. 'You wouldn't know him. He's left school.'

'Are you going with him?'

She shrugged. 'Sort of. Come closer.'

He moved closer and his knee brushed against hers. She leant towards him and smudged mascara on his cheeks and along his jaw.

'That's dirty enough,' she said and turned back to the mirror to paint her lips bright red.

They went out and stood with Tammy on the side of the stage and took turns peeping through a join in the curtain.

'That's my mum and dad,' said Margie. 'In the second row. The woman with the white cardigan.'

The dark-haired woman was reading her program. Beside her, Margie's two sisters were laughing, talking and waving to people rows behind them. On the far side, in the middle of the hall, was

Nan, sitting quietly, watching the stage.

Tammy tugged at his arm. 'Look,' she said and pointed to where Tom, Trisha and Danny stood near the back door. 'I didn't think they'd come.'

'Me neither.'

'Are you nervous?'

Mick nodded. 'Tammy, I'm sorry I didn't come round that day. To practise with you.'

She was looking at the floor. 'That's all right.'

'I mean it. Are you . . . are you going to the party at Mark's place? The one after the last show?'

'I don't know.'

'Penny said she'd drive us all home.'

'Are you going?'

Mick nodded.

'I'll ask Mum. I reckon she'll let me.'

Tammy pointed out her parents and her younger brother and then Mick looked again at the still form of his grandmother.

The workhouse kids and the Londoners, their make-up done, their costumes checked, crowded around, giggling, till Mr Richards came and shooed them out. He winked at Tammy, Mick and Margie. 'You stars can stay. Just don't let yourselves be seen by your fans.'

The hall was almost full. Mrs Pine and her husband and a handful of important-looking people came down to the front row. Margie pointed out the photographer from the paper and the reporter standing at the side. Masterman, dressed in a cream suit, still wearing his sunglasses, strode down the centre aisle and stopped a few rows from the front. He looked around as if choosing the right person to sit with and the best place for a view of the whole stage.

The boy's a bludger, I wouldn't have him on any team of mine.

Stuff you, Masterman. You'd better be watching. I am here, Michael Jamieson. He closed the gap in the curtain.

'Come on. Penny says we have to meet out the back.' Alan touched him lightly on the back of the head. 'How's the stomach?'

'Kangaroos have stopped – I'm just petrified now. What if they don't like it?'

'They'll chuck tomatoes,' said Alan. 'Least we won't starve.'

Mick pulled the back of his shirt out of the top of his pants and left the tail flapping as he jumped off the stage. He turned and held his hand out to Tammy as she bunched up her skirt and slid down beside him.

The whole cast was gathered on the grass behind the hall. Penny stood on the back step and clapped her hands.

'OK. Quiet there. I'm doing the last-minute pep talk because Bella's gone in to start the music. Listen carefully. I've still got a cold and can't speak very loudly. It's ten minutes to curtain up. I want you to settle down and spend that time thinking about your role. Ssh. Close your eyes. Think who you are, how you hold your body, what to do with your arms, your head, how you feel.'

She paused and let silence settle over them.

'Remember everything we said at the dress rehearsal yesterday. Don't worry about any mistakes you made then. You won't make them again. If you do make a blue – don't worry. Keep going. Help each other.'

Mick took a deep breath. The churning sensation left him. He was both calm and bursting with energy.

Penny went on. 'Think of all the work we've put into this. All the work you've done. All of you. However it goes, we've all had a good time and I'm, or rather we're very proud to have worked with you. And I do mean all of you.'

He was the Dodger. When the cue came he would leap, tumble, punch the air, lead the boys, flatter Nancy, sing and sing and sing.

'Time's up,' called Mr Richards.

'As we say in the theatre,' said Penny, 'break a leg.'

He stood at the foot of the stage steps and waited. The opening chorus finished and the workhouse kids came pushing and stumbling through the back of the set.

'Ssh,' hissed Mr Richards. 'Ssh. They'll hear you.'

The deep voice of Mr Bumble echoed through the hall, Tammy's voice too in their duet. Mick followed the whole song, concentrating, willing her not to miss a word or a note.

'She's singing well,' whispered Penny. 'It's a great audience. They're laughing in all the right places. No mistakes so far.' She stood silently beside Mick as the next two songs continued. 'You ready?'

He nodded.

He went up the steps and when he got to the wings, turned back to the tiny group that was watching. Margie winked and waved a clenched fist in the air, Penny grinned and Alan rubbed his hands together, stooped like Fagin. Tammy had come off the stage and stood behind them, holding up crossed fingers. Mick winked at her, put his hands on his hips, swaggered, tossed a thumb into the air and somersaulted through the wings onto the stage.

The audience clapped and cheered but he didn't hear them. He leapt and turned, beckoned to Oliver, charmed him and led him to Fagin's den. He paraded across the stage, the rest of the gang behind him, singing in a voice so startling and so rich that those in the audience who knew him turned to the person next to them, commenting in surprise.

Mick saw none of this. He kowtowed to Fagin and bowed to Nancy. He ignored the sweat pouring off his forehead. He puffed out his chest. This was the feeling that Margie talked of. Better than trophies. Better than winning. Maybe Tom and Danny felt this way in a grand final. It was magic. Great. He stepped back while Alan moved to the centre of the stage for his song. He caught his breath then, looking out into the audience for Nan, but the lighting was so low that he couldn't make out where she was.

The music started for the final song of the act. Alan, as Fagin, was singing with Mick leading the chorus. Mick jumped from the staircase to the table.

> 'It's him that pays the piper,
> It's us that plays the tune . . .'

He danced on the table. The gang surged beneath him. Alan sang the second verse. Then Mick led them in.

'And when we're in the distance . . . '

No. That was the final chorus.

Don't stop. Can't go back. If you make a mistake, keep going.

'You'll hear this . . . '

Bella, on the piano, hesitated for a note and then went with him. Margie stopped for less than a second, caught his eye and then continued her stride to the back of the stage. The gang never missed a beat.

I'm getting it wrong.

'So long, faredy well, pip pip cheerio
We'll be back soon.'

I stuffed it up.

The audience was clapping and cheering. Their hands held high in front of their faces.

I let her down.

Mick looked across the faces for Nan. He saw only Masterman.

The boy's a bludger. He'll let you down.

The curtain fell.

Mick ran from the stage. Margie reached out to hug him but he ran past her, past the smiling faces and outstretched arms of the rest of the cast, past Tammy and Penny at the foot of the steps. He ran along the narrow corridor past the change room and the kitchen. At the back door he stopped. He looked out into the darkness and then back into the warmth and light.

'Mick! Mick!' Penny's voice.

Then Margie's and Mr Richards'.

There was another tiny room tacked onto the end of the building. Behind him came clapping and laughter.

'Mick! Mick!'

He ducked into the laundry, slammed the door and threw himself under the cold cement tubs.

Cool. Dark. Spider smell. Hard cement floor. He wedges himself into the space. His nose presses against the rough brick wall. Clapping sounds ring in his ears. I've let you down. No one's put a foot wrong. I made a mistake. He rolls over and his face is almost on the floor . . . you repay me like this . . . you let me down . . . Doors slam. Loud voices. A no good bludger . . . a boy like that will only let you down . . . He screws his eyes tightly closed, wraps his arms around his chest. His body rocks . . . *Don't let me down, Mick. It's up to you to look after Mum . . . She's dead, Mick. You can't see her. It'd upset you . . . thin hand, green dressing gown, waves at the window . . . the funeral'll take a couple of hours . . . let you down.*

Mum. Penny.

He bashes his head down on the floor. Mum dead. Her head hurt. Blood runs from his forehead. *Bring me the medicine, Mick. Bring* . . . Down and down. I'm sorry. I'm sorry. I'm sorry.

The door opens. Penny sits on the floor beside him. She reaches out her hand and touches his back.

'Why don't you let it all out, Mick?' she says softly.

His body shakes. Then hot tears pour down his cheeks.

Fifteen

He is under the laundry tubs, curled up like a baby. He has bashed his face against the cold cement floor and the blood has run from a cut on his forehead. I want my mother. But he does not say it out loud. He tries to see her face but he sees only the white hands clutching the dressing gown across her chest. The pink nail polish is chipped. Her black leather watchband is almost falling off her thin wrist.

'Go away.'

'No.'

Mick's shoulders heave under her hand. He speaks again and the words come out all mixed up with sobs and sounds that come from deep within him. 'You shouldn't've put me in it. I never wanted to do it. You knew this'd happen.'

'Knew what'd happen?'

'That I'd wreck it.'

'You haven't wrecked it.'

'I let you down.'

'No you didn't.'

'I did so. I do it all the time. Everyone.'

Be good while we're gone. You're not coming to the church, Dad tells Mick. It's not a place for kids. Stay home and Mrs Jackson will stay with you. Don't leave me, Dad. Don't go away. When he's gone, the woman comes to find

139

*him. She is on the floor stretching her arms out to him.
Come on out, she says. Come on out and have a good cry,
it'll do you good. He pushes back closer to the wall. People
come for a cup of tea. Come on out, Dad says. When Mick
doesn't reply he looks like he might get angry but then
shrugs his shoulders and goes away and Mick doesn't
come out until after everyone has gone home and he is
hungry. The blood on his forehead is dry and brown.*

'Mick.' Penny takes her hand away and shifts
position to make herself more comfortable. 'I don't
feel let down. You made a mistake. Anyone
could've done that.'

'But no one did.' He trembles and his face is hot
despite the cold wind blowing in under the door. He
smells dust and oil rags and he can feel cobwebs
brushing against his cheek.

'That's where you're wrong.'

'Who did? I'm the only one.'

'No. Margie missed a line after her first entrance,'
says Penny. 'You didn't notice, did you? And if you
didn't notice that, you can understand that no one
noticed your mistake. Only those of us up there with
you and we're not judging. The audience is loving
every minute. I meant what I said before – I'm so
proud of you.'

'I'm not going back on.'

Penny doesn't answer. She stays where she is,
leaning back against the tub. After a few minutes she
speaks again. 'Who did you mean by "everyone"?'

'You know . . . Masterman.'

'Does that bother you?'

'Not really.'

'Who else?'

'I'm not telling.'

'Mick, we all make mistakes. Even the worst ones can be put behind us. They don't stay with us forever.'

Dad comes back. I'm sorry, says Mick. I tried to stop them taking her to hospital. If she had stayed home she would've been all right, I could've looked after her. It's all right, son, says Dad, but his eyes are red and he sits for a long time, not talking. He has left the truck in Townsville and will have to go and pick it up after the funeral.

'Three months ago,' says Penny, 'I cast you in the play because I thought you were the right person for the part. Nothing that has happened since has made me change my mind. Not the business with the model. Not the problem when you missed rehearsal. We got through those all right. You were then and you are now absolutely the right person for it.'

Mick rolls onto his side and looks towards her. His throat is dry and his head hurts. He is still trembling. She is a shadowy outline. He could reach out and touch her.

'I can't go back on.'

'You can and you will. Tammy's out there and Margie, worried and waiting for you.'

'You don't know . . . '

'If you told me, I might be able to help.'

'I don't know. I can't stop thinking.'

'Is it to do with your father?'

'Sort of. Him and Mum. But I never think about

141

them. I don't want to think about them.' Mum, Dad, Nan, Tom, the waitress at the truckstop, Masterman being horrible. Mr Richards who is not horrible, Margie who doesn't care, Tammy who, maybe . . .

'I want you to listen to me, Mick.' Penny reaches down and covers one of his hands with her own. She speaks quickly. 'We've got ten more minutes before you have to go back on. I am saying "we" because you know all that stuff about the risks we took. If we fail now, then Bella and I fail too. And Margie, Tammy, David, Mark and Alan. All of us. Whatever is going on with you has been stewing for a long time. It's not just what happened up there on stage, it's part of you. You've kept a lid on it till now. You can do it again. Block it off for the moment. Get up there with the others and finish what we started. But it won't go away and I promise you now, we will deal with it.'

Mick moves slightly towards her. 'What do you mean?'

'I mean that after this show is over, you and I are going to sit down and have a long talk about . . . about all sorts of things.'

'No. I can't do it.' He pulls his hand away.

'Mick, I want to tell you something that I haven't told anyone else. I wrote a letter about a week ago to a friend of mine. In it I told her I planned to quit teaching.'

He pushes himself up on one arm. 'What?'

'I said I'd had enough, I wasn't suited any more and I was quitting at the end of the term and going away. Tonight, for a number of reasons, I've changed my mind. I'm going to be around after this play. I've got too much unfinished business.' She looks at him intently. 'There's lots I could say. But we're on in a few minutes. You're not in the opening number. You've got time to get yourself ready.' She leans forward and touches his cheek. 'I'll see you out there, Dodger.'

She is gone. He is cold. He tries to sit up but he knocks his head on the cement tub. Footsteps run past the door. Piano music comes softly from the hall. He scratches the caked blood on his forehead. Unfinished business.

He is ten years old. Dad has gone north with a load. I'll be three days away. You look after her. Don't let me down. She is in the bedroom. Her head hurts. She is sick. She grips the end of the blanket in her thin hands and cries out. The nurse comes and is angry. He shouldn't have gone and left you, she says to both of them. Mum tries to make a joke but her face twists and she is sick again. They call Mrs Jackson from across the road and an ambulance for the hospital. He rides in the back with Mum and she holds his hand. He doesn't want to let her go but he wants to sit in the front so that kids from school can see he is there, riding in the ambulance with the siren blaring. She gives him her watch and says she won't be needing it in hospital. Where's your father? the doctor says but Mick can't tell him which town he was headed for and by the time the police find him she is dead. Dead at night, while he is sleeping in Mrs Jackson's spare room. They didn't tell me she was that sick, is all he says to her when she wraps her arms around him and says, Your mum is gone, lovey. She's dead. He sits perfectly still. She is dead. He cannot

143

see her. He cannot touch her, be held by her. Inside his head is empty. The world is empty. He can do nothing. Is nothing. He cannot even remember her face.

Mick crawls into the centre of the room and stands up. The light from the street lamp comes through the cracked glass window. The music out in the hall grows louder. His arms and legs feel stiff and heavy. He shakes them, slowly and deliberately. Then he rolls his head and drops his shoulders. He bends at the waist and bounces the top half of his body.

Unfinished business. They'll be standing behind the curtain. Margie ready to start her song. Penny is wrong. He isn't in this one as a solo but he does have to stand beside Margie and give her his hand as she jumps up on the table to dance. She'll manage without him. Someone else will do it. But if she's missed a line before, she might get thrown by it and miss one again. He should be there. He rubs his eyes. No time to clean up. He is supposed to be dirty. Deal with it later. Everything later. He breathes deeply. The music is almost to curtain up.

He is the Dodger.

He opens the door and runs along the hall. Penny is talking to Tammy at the foot of the stairs. Their mouths drop and they move to hug him but he runs past them and leaps up onto the stage.

Dear Fran:

You're going to think I'm hopeless! I've
changed my mind again. I am not going to
resign. I am going to stick it out here for
another year. It is a bit hard to explain
why but I'll try.

I decided in the middle of the play. It was,
of course, fantastic. Everything we'd
struggled with for weeks beforehand came
together at the right moment. The kids were
great, the audience was everything you
could wish for, and it made me think
everything was worth it after all. At the
height of it I had a bit of a showdown with
Mick. The stupid idiot made a mistake and
thought he'd wrecked the whole show. He
hadn't of course - no one had even noticed,
but that didn't stop him from breaking
down and saying that he couldn't go back
on. I talked to him for a while and then
left him - not really sure if he would
actually get back up on the stage. Thank
God he did! And of course he sang
wonderfully. The audience clapped and
cheered for encore after encore. He couldn't
believe it when he took a bow and he got
all this clapping and feet stamping - just
for him. I must say I felt proud. We had a
great party afterwards at one of the kids'
houses. It was like being about eighteen

again and I wanted to dance and rage all night with my students! What would Masterman say!

Anyway – to cut a long story short. I'm staying. I do enjoy what I'm doing. It's hard for all the reasons that I mentioned before but I don't feel I can cut out so quickly. I've just organized Mick into counselling. There's a whole load of stuff going on in his head about his mother's death and his relationship with his father and although I know that no one's indispensable, I feel that I can't walk out on him now. There's also year eleven kids going on to twelve and the other thing is that Bella and I have got this great idea about a show. No more staid old musicals for us. She wants to enter the rock eisteddfod, get the kids to write a rock show and then enter it in the state-wide competition. Mick and a girl in his class called Tammy are keen – so who knows – we might just do it!

Sorry for all this raving on about the play. Now that it's finished I'll have to write about more esoteric things like love (?) and the meaning of life! I hope I haven't caused any problems for your plans with all my chopping and changing. I think it's the right thing to do – correction – I <u>know</u> it is.

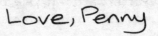

Love, Penny

Dad's place

Dear penny
                    how are you?
I'm fine.
It's hot. Me and Dad
went fishing yesterday.
you know that stuff Mr
Malcolm said I have to
do - well ~~you~~ Dad said
it was stupid but he
took me to the cemetery
and he showed me the
grave and then he
cleared out. I'm not
scared of ghosts or
anything but it was
real spooky. Mr Malcom
said talk to her. I
couldn't I thought about
it, and the play, and
how great it was - like
at the end when
everyone was stomping
and cheering - even Tom
and Trisha. And about

you and Tammy and
margie and mark. I
couldn't talk out loud
to someone who wasn't
there. But then this
weird thing happened.
I sang a song, the one
I do with margie. It
just came out and I
sang it right through
to the end.
   Promise you won't
tell. Not even Tammy.
   I'm coming back next
week. Dad's got a load. We'll
drive all night.
   Do we have to wait
till next year before we
start on The rock
musical? Tammy wrote me
a letter and she's got
all These ideas already
   See you later.

   Mick
   P.S. I'm glad you'r staying

Also in Puffin

ELEANOR, ELIZABETH
Libby Gleeson

Eleanor has been wary of her new home so far: the landscape's strange, the faces in the classroom unfriendly. Then, unexpectedly, her lonely new life changes — with the discovery of her grandmother's old diary. Now, with a bush fire rampaging just behind them, her life and the lives of Ken, Mike and six-year-old Billy depend on how she uses what she *has* learned about this alien world. She needs help, and only her grandmother, sixty-five years away, can give it to her.

THE CUCKOO CHILD
Dick King-Smith

This is the story of Oliver, an ostrich taken as an egg from a safari park and fostered by a pair of increasingly confused geese. What are they to make of their beloved but most un-goose-like son? The lad can't even swim! But he can run — and run faster than anyone in the farmyard could ever dream. And this gives Jack an idea. Imagine a ride on such a creature!

THE MARSHMALLOW EXPERIMENT
Rachel Dixon

Jo is puzzled by Abednego, the extraordinary magician at the fair who seems to pay him special attention. But when his friend Gemma gets into trouble for the disappearance of a rabbit from her mother's pet shop, they both suspect that Abednego is responsible and set out to find him.

Tracking him down proves harder than they expect, and when they do, Abednego reveals that he has been testing their suitability for an unbelievable experiment.

HAUNTING TALES
ed. Barbara Ireson

Ghost stories have an endless fascination for writers and young reader alike, and here in this collection are some of the very best, by famous writers like H. G. Wells, Arthur Conan Doyle, E. Nesbit, Joan Aiken and Ray Bradbury.

GHOSTLY GALLERY
ed. Alfred Hitchcock

Ten eerie encounters – or half encounters – take place in this bumper collection of ghost stories. Some of the tales are not too serious, some are even funny, but most are spooky and spine-chilling. What else would you expect when they were chosen by Alfred Hitchcock, master of the macabre?

JASON BODGER AND THE PRIORY GHOST
Gene Kemp

When Jason Bodger, school menace and student teacher's nightmare, visits a priory with Class 4Z, he has a most peculiar and disturbing experience. He sees a strange girl walking towards him high up on a non-existent beam, Mathilda de Chetwynde, born in a castle over 700 years ago, has decided that Jason is just the person she's been waiting for – and there's not a thing Jason can do about it!

NAPPER GOES FOR GOAL

Martin Waddell

Napper McCann and the star players of Red Row Primary School start a football team and imagine a glorious, successful future. But then they discover how hard it is to win games. A funny and exciting story with plenty of illustrations and diagrams for football fans.

THE BEST-KEPT SECRET

Emily Rodda

The arrival of the fairground carousel, surrounded by its neat red and white painted fence, with a tent guarding its entrance, was a complete mystery to the residents of Marley Street. Where had it come from? How had it appeared so quickly? And why was the music so haunting, beckoning all to come and look? Jo is determined to have a ride, even though she senses the ride may take her into danger, into an unknown world . . . the world of the future.

SKYLARK

K. M. Peyton

Life isn't much fun for Ben – until he meets Elf and is drawn into an exciting adventure. But the two children must keep their secret from the thoughtless adults in this delightful and touching story. He wished he was brave, like boys in books, but the fact was . . . he was hating every minute of his adventure.

MAN IN MOTION

Jan Mark

Once Lloyd has started at his new school, he soon finds he's playing cricket with Salman, swimming with Kenneth, cycling with James and playing badminton with Vlad. But American football is Lloyd's greatest enthusiasm. And in time it tests his loyalties, not only to his other sporting activities, but also to the new friends he shares them with.

THE OUTSIDE CHILD

Nina Bawden

Imagine suddenly discovering you have a step-brother and -sister no one has ever told you about! It's the most exciting thing that's ever happened to Jane, and she can't wait to meet them. Perhaps at last she will become part of a 'proper' family, instead of for ever being the outside child. So begins a long search for her brother and sister, but when she finally does track them down, Jane finds there are still more surprises in store!

THE FOX OF SKELLAND

Rachel Dixon

Samantha's never liked the old custom of Foxing Day – the fox costume especially gives her the creeps. So when Jason and Rib, children of the new publicans at The Fox and Lady, find the costume and Jason wears it to the fancy-dress disco, she's sure something awful will happen.

Then Sam's old friend Joseph sees the ghost of the Lady and her fox. Has she really come back to exact vengeance on the village? Or has her appearance got something to do with the spate of burglaries in the area?